I0659145

Love Reborn

Cascade Bay, Volume 1

Solara Gordon

Published by THE EARTH MOVED, LLC, 2021.

LOVE REBORN

First edition. May 21, 2021.

Copyright © 2021 Solara Gordon.

ISBN: 978-1737305910

Written by Solara Gordon.

Also by Solara Gordon

Cascade Bay
Love Reborn

Standalone
A Heart's Desire
To Love You Again
To Love You Again

Watch for more at https://solaragordon.com/.

Cascade Bay
Love Reborn

Torrey Neadson wants love, connection and the white-picket fence. She blew the chance at having it with Holt, once.

Holt Addison is through with one-night stands. Problem is Torrey moved on before he could tell her.

Stranded together by a freak coastal storm, they recognize what their hearts crave and hungers demand. Has distance and time undone the strength of what they once had?

Genre: Contemporary

Length: 53,358 words

DEDICATION

First drafts are for the author. Our story resonates deep inside us, waiting to leap on to the page. Sometimes, the characters dictate their story and we, the author, take on the role of the scribe. When both of these merge together, something magical occurs. Add in readers and more magic happens. I'm blessed with a reader group, Solara's Glamorous Stars, who share their opinions, reading preferences, and suggestions as part of my writing process.

The following list helped with titling Torrey and Holt's story. A special thank-you goes to: Christine Heydt, Tilya Eloff, Maggie Keiko, Chandra Woolson, Patricia Nelson, Chevy Allen, Tina Evans Atkinson, Terri Pray, Tammy Layton, Chris Roberts, Deborah Dawkins, Barbara Burdette, Teresa Padgett, Ann Waters, Denise Leitch-Gaff, Janet Ludlow Bunnell, Dina Stronello, Joyce Mintzas, Tracy Harrison, Lisa Hosenfeld, Amanda Hash, Kris Rubi, Patricia Centivre, Sylvia Dominick, Liz Deshayes, Jennifer Kayes, Crystal LeClair, Brenda Chambers, Linda Rimer-Como, Kathy Brown, Carol Sigle Doscher, Nicki Mech, Julia Richardson, Allyson Abu-Hajar, Julie Bryant, and Jill Cerniglia.

Chapter One

"You told Joanna I'd sleep with Torrey?" Holt Addison winced as his voice echoed over the last strains of music blaring from the speakers near the dance floor. The din of McClark's patrons hushed as though everyone listened, waiting to catch his next utterance.

Holt set down his half-full beer bottle. He turned slowly on his stool until he faced his best friend and culprit, Stuart Doxson. Patrons moved off the dance floor as servers made their way through the congested table-and-chair section of the dining area. Low-key music began playing in the background.

Holt tugged his beer to him. He swallowed a third of it before placing the bottle back on the bar. He motioned Stuart closer.

"I'm gonna ask you once. Why?" Holt crossed his arms tight against his chest. As much as he didn't want to lose his cool, Stuart's shrug didn't help.

"Come on, Stuart. I understand you got it bad for Joanna. But telling her that I'd sleep with Torrey is going too far." Holt shook his head. He ran his hands through his short hair, knowing it only made his hair stand up more. He wished his conscience would stop flashing a familiar, feminine, sexually-flushed-face through his mind.

Stuart knew how much he hated being set up and blind dates. He'd rather go dateless than spend time making pleasant idle chatter with someone he knew little about. Tonight Stuart trumped himself.

Stuart attracted women like moths to a flame. His rugged chin, goatee, red hair, and boyish grin stood out against his light tan. At six foot one, Stuart drew attention to himself without trying. His brown eyes lit up as he smiled.

Joanna Angstrom nudged her business partner, Torrey Neadson, as they sat two tables over from the bar area. "There's Stuart. I wonder if Holt is with him. You love his blue eyes and wonderful smile. And those black silky curls of his...oh, mama, one hottie!"

Torrey sighed, fighting hard to keep from rolling her eyes. Why had she agreed to accompany Joanna? Joanna's zeal to see Stuart again barely exceeded her graphic details of the gossip her cohorts dished out on Holt's sexual prowess.

"Joanna, I don't care how many times Holt can do it in a night. Nor how long his cock is or which girls he's done." Torrey looked down, working her jaw up and down. Gritting her teeth did no good. Joanna smiled and nodded. She had it bad for Stuart. Not that Torrey blamed Joanna. She and Stuart looked good together. Torrey hoped Holt hadn't agreed with them to join her for dinner and a night of sexual pleasure.

"But, Torrey—" Joanna started. Torrey shot her hand up, ready to clap it over Joanna's mouth if she blurted out another sexual comment concerning Holt as if it were the lead story on the evening news.

Joanna nodded as Torrey shook her head. "Joanna, I'm as sex positive as you are. I don't need every piece of sexual gossip you've heard about Holt."

"Well, how are you going to know if he's still good in bed or not?" Joanna waved to a server at the table next to theirs.

Torrey refrained from answering until the server left with their drink order. "I'm sure I can find out on my own if *I* decide to pursue his offer if he makes me one. I need chemistry. It's not like they're nude and I'm merely shopping based on their cock size."

"Right and we don't own a lingerie and sex toy store." Joanna's offhand tone and reply sent Torrey into a coughing fit. Damn, she'd forgotten how Joanna loved puns and innuendo. Her ironical sense of humor was in full gear.

Torrey sipped her rum and cola, pretending to study the menu in front of her. Yes, they owned Ladies' Satisfaction, one of the oldest sex-oriented businesses in Cascade Bay. Just because her satisfaction came from a vibrator didn't mean she'd given up on real sex. Doing it for the sake of enjoyment was good, but after while it rang hollow for her. She wanted and needed more. Her last fling lasted six months. The one before that lasted eight weeks. Both were over a year ago. No matter how attractive she found a guy, until she connected with them beyond mutual lust, she preferred her non-pursuit status. Blast Holt for spoiling this for her.

Holt bit into his thick burger and chewed. Stuart shook Tabasco sauce into of chili before adding corn chips and stirring. How the man ate ood he did without indigestion amazed Holt. His eyes watered art shovel two large bites into his mouth.

Stuart chased his spicy mouthful with several swallows of beer before he faced him. He hoped Stuart didn't plan to pick up where their conversation left off. Way his luck was running, he didn't believe for a second Stuart would let things drop.

"Joanna knows you and Torrey were friends with benefits for a while. Since Torrey hasn't scored in a bit either, we decided getting you together made sense." Stuart grinned, saluted Holt with his beer, and glanced over his shoulder.

Holt swallowed and nodded. "What Torrey and I were to each other is in the past and between her and me. I've said it before, and I'm saying it again. I can get my own women."

"Yeah, right. How many women have you laid in the past year?" Stuart asked.

"When did you start keeping score?" Holt swallowed the last of his beer.

"Since you got grumpy and started hanging out at the gym more. I don't care how many, bro. If you were choosing to be celibate, I wouldn't care."

Holt eyed Stuart. The man had a knack for cutting to the chase. He stated the obvious.

Holt finished his burger, wiped his mouth, and gestured to the bartender for another beer. "I appreciate the concern. Speaking for me is another thing. Torrey and I might not have the *zing,* as you call it, anymore. What about what she wants? Remember when everyone kept trying to set you and Joanna up? Nothing worked out until you got together on your own."

Stuart tossed his napkin in the bowl. "Those jalapenos are wildfire tonight. Gotta tell Tony to ease up on them. I'm quitting while I can. Whoosh!" Stuart rubbed his forehead with his sweaty beer bottle.

Holt chortled. "Yes, Grandma Getty's chili got you sweating and swearing. Damn good chili as we used to say. Back to setting me up, bro. Please let Torrey and me handle it from here."

"Okay, I guess. Joanna is expecting you to sweep Torrey off her feet and into your bedroom."

"I'm not seducing her and fleeing. I gave up one-night stands. Shallow and hollow isn't what I'm looking for anymore." Holt dropped his share of the tab on the bar. "When are they supposed to arrive? I'd like to give Torrey the once-over before she sees me."

Stuart picked up his beer and pointed. "See the blonde in the low-cut top standing near the table over there? You can't have missed the cleavage."

Holt rolled his eyes and smiled. Stuart's heart was committed, but his libido kept on shopping. "Which way to the right or left of her?"

Stuart stood. "They're to the left and back a table. Joanna is facing us."

Holt squinted, covering his eyes. He blinked. His contacts burned. He'd forgotten his glasses at work. He hadn't had time to find the spare pair he kept in his gym bag. Stuart had tossed both bags in the trunk of his car as they left the gym.

Holt caught a glimpse of Torrey as the server turned. He hadn't seen her in two years. He remembered her azure eyes and smile. How much had she changed? Their heated passion had lasted a brief period. The last he'd heard from her, she'd started a new relationship and wished him well. Guess that hadn't worked out.

He smiled as Torrey turned around. He liked the new short spikey haircut she wore. Her heart-shaped face and full lips stood out. Even the animated way she acted and laughed with Joanna spoke volumes about what his sister, Gwen, had told him. The shy reserved Torrey he had known was gone. She'd changed in ways that empowered her to strike out on her own and open a business few women would dare to contemplate. She seemed to be envisioning something as she talked with the guy standing next to her. It was as though she beamed when she replied. Confidence certainly became her. There was no doubt she genuinely smiled. Her eyes appeared to glow as she stood and hugged the server closest to her.

Warmth exploded in Holt's groin and leapt upward. The blast threatened to overtake his feigned composure. Confident women turned him on. Always had, and yet with Torrey there was more. He'd fallen for her without knowing or seeing this side of her. Her gentle kindness and giving heart had snagged him early on in their friendship. No matter how many women he dated and tried relationships with, none of them compared to Torrey. Wasn't fair to them, but he hadn't realized how deep his feelings ran. Why some other guy hadn't scooped her up was beyond him. Then again, Holt hadn't wanted Torrey exclusively then. Maybe he didn't want it now.

A jolt gripped his gut as he saw her smiling and talking with another guy. He clenched the edge of the bar to keep from fisting his hand. Torrey needed someone who understood her, accepted her, and cared about her. Certainly not some dude she'd just hooked up with.

Holt eased off his stool. He knew what he wanted. It was time Torrey realized he did and they were meant for each other. "Come on, Stuart. Let's go *claim* our dates."

Stuart watched Holt's determined stride close the distance between them and where Joanna and Torrey sat. Stuart smiled as Holt stopped their server on her way to the kitchen. A few nods later, he motioned for Stuart to catch up. Stuart shoved his hand into his pocket, pulled out a twenty, adding it to Holt's share of the tab, and sauntered across the dance floor.

Chapter Two

"I didn't order this." Torrey looked up from the large piece of double chocolate cheesecake the server placed beside the bowl of minestrone soup she'd ordered.

The server smiled and pointed. "He did." Torrey faced the direction she indicated and sighed.

"Great. Just great," she muttered, wanting to send the rich dessert back. Holt probably expected her to reject him. He thought to get to her through her sweet tooth. Torrey swallowed her further retorts, trying to avoid Joanna's all-knowing smile.

"I'd ask who your admirer is, but I believe I see him coming this way." Joanna winked and stuck out her tongue.

"Telling you something nasty would land on your tongue just somehow doesn't do my anxiety justice." Torrey pushed the cake aside. She picked up the soupspoon, filled it, and blew on the hot liquid before tasting.

"Your anxiety? Over Holt?" Joanna stood. "Good thing we're inside or lightning might get you before it hit me."

Torrey grabbed her napkin and quickly covered her mouth. Her throat burned. Her eyes watered as her nose twitched. Blast Joanna for zinging her with the one line their mothers loved to threaten them with as kids.

Torrey cleared her throat, willed herself to sip her water, before she responded. "Yes, anxiety over Holt."

"Why would you be anxious over me?" Holt's voice sounded from slightly behind her.

Loosening her grip on the glass she held, Torrey took a deep breath. She blinked, wondering why each time she did images in front of her grew hazier. Glancing up, she saw Joanna watching her intently. Had Joanna mouthed *breathe*?

Torrey opened her mouth to question what Joanna was saying. Two burps followed by a yawn caught her by surprise. So much for appearing calm and together in front of Holt. He'd already heard her admit her anxiety. Now she belched as if she lacked manners. Great, what a flop at secondary first impressions.

She inhaled and exhaled before she tried speaking again. "Isn't that a question I should be asking you?"

Holt bit the inside of his lip. Laughter threatened to spill out. He wanted to cup Torrey's face between his hands and brush his lips over hers. Her lush, full lips pouted when she felt cornered. He could see her careful moves as though she sought to hide her inner turmoil. He caught the conspiratorial wink Joanna sent Stuart. Let them think they'd pulled something off.

He hadn't forgotten one inch of Torrey's body. The way her plush breasts filled his hands as he cupped them. Or her throaty sighs as he trailed his fingers tips lightly over her engorged clit and nipples. Their need to couple had flooded heat over them every time they'd come together. Physical intimacy worked well between them. Neither had sought or asked for more than what they thought was friendship mixed with mutual lust. He knew better now. This time, he knew how deep he wanted to go and what his stakes were. Convincing Joanna and Stuart to let Torrey and him do this on their own was but one stumbling stone on the path Holt saw before him.

"Torrey, I'll admit I'm anxious. I don't think you want me to say out loud what I am uneasy about." Holt pulled out the chair closest to her and sat down. Stuart rounded the table and sat next to Joanna.

"You've gained more manners, I see." Torrey's flushed cheeks told him she'd rather not continue in the direction his thoughts were running.

"Always had them. You just never saw them enough to realize how polite and courteous I am." Holt snagged a handful of oyster crackers from the bowl in front of Torrey. He tossed several into his mouth.

"I didn't know you hadn't eaten," Stuart offered, nudging Joanna. "We got here earlier, figuring we'd meet you for dinner."

"Depends on what you call *eating* and *dinner*." Joanna's emphasis on eating and dinner left little to any of their imaginations as she continued. "Don't know about you and Torrey, Holt. I *know* who Stuart is eating for dessert, or his second course."

"Water," Holt coughed. Blast Joanna and her punning sense of humor. The cheesy grin she wore set ripples off in more places than Holt liked.

Torrey slid her glass of water in front of him. "Crackers a bit salty?" Her arched eyebrow and rolled eyes didn't help.

Holt gulped water, swallowing. He reached for a napkin. If his eyes kept watering, he'd have to leave for fear of losing a contact. Dabbing his eyes, Holt kicked Stuart under the table.

Stuart startled. Sitting upright, he glared at Holt. "What the hell was that for?"

"Sorry. I didn't mean to, you know." Holt hoped he plastered the best innocent grin he knew how to fake across his face. "Now that I have your attention, though, we could use a couple of fresh drinks. How about I buy and you get them?"

Holt tossed a twenty on the table. If Stuart didn't notice the non-verbal signals, he deserved a well-placed kick in the seat of his jeans.

Joanna claimed the twenty and rose. "Come on, Stuart. We'll get the drinks. Torrey needs a fresh one. I know I do."

Torrey glanced over her shoulder as Stuart and Joanna threaded their way through the crowd toward the bar. She turned back, facing Holt. "Why are you here?"

She kept her hands below the table. Clenching and unclenching her hands did nothing to relieve the new flutters her stomach did each time Holt's gaze ran over her. The heat rolled off him in huge waves, threatening to overwhelm her if she didn't keep her icy shield in place. Problem was her hormones had different ideas. The man knew how to read her. He'd learned how to turn her on and keep the heat going. Chemistry didn't need a catalyst with him.

"I'd ask you the same thing. Except I probably know why you're here." Holt laid his arm on the table and leaned forward. "Things didn't work out, did they?"

Torrey scooted her chair further away. Even a bit of space might allow some air in to help cool down the heat blasts boiling up between them. "I'm here because I want to be. What do you mean it didn't work out?"

Holt toyed with his napkin before his gaze met hers. She swallowed hard. His eyes smoldered the same way they had when she'd cried out his name as multiple orgasms claimed her. He wanted her just as he had then. She couldn't deny her attraction either. This time she wasn't jumping into bed with him.

"If things *had* worked out, would you be here?" Torrey cringed at Holt's emphasis on the word had. Damn, could he read her that easily? How much did he know?

"What if it hadn't? I remember you saying that no woman would tie you down. You wanted to be free to pursue what came your way. You said I could do the same." Torrey paused. Rubbing her lips together, she watched the glint in Holt's eyes dim. She gripped her hands together under the table. Apologizing would only tell him what he said was true. Before he'd started dating another woman, he'd come close to taking a good chunk of her heart and sanity. Rumors flew hot and heavy concerning his involvement with the other woman. He'd never denied the juicy tales nor did he answer her e-mails and calls asking for clarification. What right did he think he had to sit here and challenge her?

Holt leaned closer. His hand reached for hers. "Torrey, I know I said some dumb things in the past. And that line was the lamest. Truth is, two years ago I lived in the heat of the moment. The flash of passion ruled my libido."

Torrey jumped as Holt's hand brushed her arm. "Excuse me," she offered, sitting upright against the back of her chair. She voiced the question running rampant through her mind. "This has changed?"

Holt's response and smile cracked more of her icy resolve. "Yes, *I've* changed. I'm different from who you knew before. Two years is a lot of time when you're apart. Are you saying you haven't?"

Torrey looked down unable to meet the question in Holt's eyes. She needed more than just words. Could she risk taking a chance? A chance on great sex and passion? She knew Holt kept his word. But could she trust him with her heart?

Chapter Three

Three hours later

"I swear we were set up." Torrey pulled her sweater tighter around her and sank lower in the warm leather seat in Holt's car. "Joanna's car started fine when we left the store."

Holt's snicker drew her attention. He glanced at her before returning to concentrating on his driving. "If we were, so what? At least, Stuart and Joanna aren't here. I'm glad it's you and me."

Torrey fidgeted with her seat belt. Did she dare admit she agreed with him? "It's a lot quieter for sure."

She caught Holt's smiling reflection as he drove under a streetlight. Rain pounded against the windshield. Only the swish of the wipers cleared the window before more drops pelted the glass. Without preamble, the storm had rolled in off the bay, catching them in its wake as they exited McClark's. Neither Joanna nor Stuart thought to prepare ahead. Torrey hadn't heard the weather forecast either. Now she sat in wet clothing, praying she didn't chill before Holt got her home.

Torrey lurched in her seat as Holt twisted the steering wheel violently left and right. "Shit, hold tight. I'll see if we can dodge the cop car."

Torrey squinted as blue and red flashing lights pierced through the rain. Sounds of tires skidding and cussing filled the air. She groped for the door handle, praying they stopped in time. Closing her eyes, she prayed harder. Her fingernails cut tight against her palms. Her heart skipped one beat, then two. A hollow thud sounded, and she swayed back and forth in her seat for several moments.

"Damn, what a place to pull someone over," Holt fussed. "Stay put while I see if we did more than tap his bumper."

Holt opened his door carefully after checking approaching traffic in the side and rearview mirrors. Wind surged against the door, threatening to pull it out of his hand. Rain pelted his face, trickling in streams down his cheeks and forehead. He wiped his face against his shoulder, hoping to keep the water out of his eyes. It was bad enough driving with gritty contacts in. Burning and itchy he could do without.

Gripping the door firmer, Holt eased his way out of the car. In between wind bursts, he could make out the flashing lights of the police car in front of him. He closed the door and moved along the car with his back against the frame. He didn't want to lose sight of the lights from any car speeding down the road. As he reached the headlights, he blinked and his night vision kicked in. Three figures stood near the car stopped in front of the cruiser. Three flat tires along with the precarious way the car hung over a narrow roadside ditch spoke volumes. The three were lucky. Someone watched over them. A head turned toward him. Next, a flashlight shined in his face.

Holt raised his arm, trying to block the brightest part of the beam. "Can you lower that, please?"

"Sorry, sir. You can't be too careful on a night like this." Gravel crunched under the officer's feet as he approached. "How can I help you?"

A woman with two small children followed the officer. Their haggard, tired faces illuminated each time the blue strobe came back around. The children clutched their mother's hand as though fear poured out of them. The woman's hair hid her face. Holt hoped help was there for them. Too many lost folks got left behind more than he liked. Reaching into his pocket, he pulled out a few bills and one of the business cards he kept handy. The shelter could house them for a bit. He'd check with his sister in the morning. Her job as the head social worker would give him the information he needed to assist more.

"We skidded to a stop due to the severe weather. I hit your bumper. Didn't want problems." Holt moved away from the headlights, closer to the officer.

The officer arced the flashlight's beam over the bumper of the cruiser and back to Holt's car. "Not anything. You nudged the rubber portion we use to help stop folks. No problem. If you're going farther, you need to turn back. Old Mill Creek Road is under water. They've evacuated the shoreline, too."

Holt cussed under his breath. He'd have to take the long way back to Torrey's place. She'd given him her address after he said he'd call Joanna or Stuart for it. The way back to his place would take more time as he would have to double back to avoid Shoreline Drive due to the evacuation.

Wind swirled around them, pushing Holt tight against his car. He glanced toward the woman and children. Their wet clothes clung to them like second skins. The children huddled closer to her. She shoved a hand through her hair. Holt sucked in air. Two dark-colored bruises adorned her cheek, and a darker area rimmed her eye. Another abuse victim. Yes, the shelter would take them. He'd make sure no one outside of the courts and law enforcement knew where they were.

"Officer," Holt began, moving closer. "Here's some money for them. Take them to the address on the card. Ask for Gwen. Tell her, her big brother says hello."

The officer took the card, carefully holding it as he read the print by flashlight. "Oh yes. I know the place. Gwen's a sweetie. She'll take good care of them. Thanks! I'll give her the money."

Holt worked his way back to his door. He glanced over his shoulder as the officer settled the woman and children in the back of his car. He loaded three supermarket plastic bags into his trunk. Holt shook his head. He hoped things worked out for them. He'd do what he could to ensure their abuser got what he deserved. He'd take their case pro bono, making sure they got the legal representation they needed.

Torrey watched Holt's actions in between swishes of the wiper blades. She couldn't help but notice his stiff posture once the woman's face came into view. Torrey slowly moved her hand away from her mouth. Harsh economic conditions brought out the best and worse in people. This woman rated respect and dignity. Someone had tossed those away and beaten her. Praise be, they were getting help. She hoped Holt asked where they were going. She wanted to follow up with as much support as she could. Ladies' Satisfaction Foundation would front any monetary help they needed. Torrey made a mental note to contact Holt's sister Gwen in the morning. She'd know where to find the family.

Torrey jumped as Holt pulled his door open. Rain blew in across his seat and onto her. "Come on. Hurry up. I prefer my showers warm, thank you."

Holt's warm laugh filled the space between them as he hastily shut the door behind him. "Like I'm going to stand out there in an ice-cold rain myself." His hand cupped her cheek. He leaned closer. Smiling, he winked.

Torrey licked her lips, unsure if she should give into her growing need. Her eyes began to close.

"Oh, honey. I would love to pull you into my arms and stir up some heat. But..."

Torrey pulled back. Her eyes shot open. "What?" Her tone surprised her. Gone was her edgy harsh voice. In its place, a softer, huskier one replaced it.

Holt dropped his hand. "Looks like we're either at my place or yours. Water is rising, and the way to either is going to take longer than we'd like."

Torrey gulped. Straightening up in her seat, she peered out the windshield. What a choice—Holt at her place or her at his.

Chapter Four

"I know a back way to my place near the store." Torrey turned slightly.

Holt nodded as he started the car. "If we turn around and take the next right, we'll get back to Main Street."

"The store is on Second Road near the courthouse and the park." Torrey shrugged as Holt glanced at her. "What's with the grin?"

Holt held up his hand. "Nothing. I never expected to be at your place. Much less see you again."

Torrey settled back in her seat. "I know. Unusual for sure."

"Maybe fate has plans for us?" Holt wished they'd gotten together on their own. He bet she felt pressured like he did. He hoped she would relax once they got to her place.

Holt concentrated on the view of the road he could see between splashes and swipes of the blades rapidly clearing the windshield of the wet onslaught. Jagged bolts of lightning illuminated the sky briefly and disappeared. Loud claps of thunder sounded. A lone streetlight here and there provided a smattering of light that did nothing to show the street names as they passed. Thank god, he knew this part of town. His office suite occupied a high-rise in the City Centre Towers near the main square in town that ran along the north end of Main Street. The drive to work usually took him thirty minutes in good traffic and over forty-five minutes at rush hour. He glanced at the dashboard clock. Twenty minutes and three side roads had passed, with possibly ten more to go before he reached what he estimated might be the turn he needed.

"Can you make out any of the street names or signs?" Holt asked, swerving to miss a low sagging tree limb buffeted by stronger wind bursts as the intensity of the rain increased. He eased off the gas pedal and gingerly applied the brake as another gust wobbled the car back and forth, forcing them closer to the other lane and into on any oncoming traffic.

He caught Torrey's movement out of the corner of his eye. Her hand rose, covered with part of her sweater sleeve, she swabbed at the window. "I can see bits and pieces. We haven't passed Main yet."

"Good, at this rate, we're going to be a while before we get there." Holt gripped the steering wheel tighter and urged his thoughts to prayers for a fleeting second. They might need all the help they could get if the storm intensified. "If you see Main before I do, let me know."

"Sur—re." Torrey's further movements kept his attention. The dim interior light allowed him to easily see her. A quick glance showed she chafed her arms. Her hair clung to her head as though she'd slicked it back. Lord, she must be wetter than he originally thought.

"I wish I could turn up the heat. But the windows will fog up. Sorry, I can't." Torrey's soft "I know" hit him midsection, hard and deep. As much as he wanted to pull over and get her into his arms, now wasn't the time. Too much weighed on them getting to safety and out of this frigging storm.

Another fifteen minutes clicked by as Holt noticed each change of the clock as he kept glancing from side to side, using what painted lines he could make out to keep them in their lane. Splashes hit the window harder each time he over steered the narrow path he could make out in front of him. Shit, water was ponding faster and deeper than he anticipated. Time to find Main Street was now. Holt squinted as a half-bent sign illumined by the car's lights came into view. Praise be, they'd made it.

Holt eased into the right turn, praying the change in direction would afford him some ease from the wind. "How far down do we need to go before we get to Second?"

"In this, I'd say three large buildings and an open parking lot. It'll be a left. I'll keep watch on this side." Torrey hunched forward in her seat.

Holt heaved a deep sigh, and gave the car more gas. A dark, eerie feeling settled over him. Not one streetlight greeted them as they slowly made their way down Main Street. The darkness outside crept up to the car, threatening to plunge them into its depths.

"Okay, we just passed the bank and city hall. What can you make out?" The pitch in Torrey's voice edged Holt's angst a few notches higher. She'd cleared her throat before she spoke the last couple of times. Her hoarse tone plus her sneezes indicated her chills were racking her more than she let on. At least, for now, she wasn't stuttering and hugging her wet sweater to her.

"I see a large dark space. I assume that's the parking lot. Right?" Holt pumped the brake to slow down and keep from skidding.

"Yes. You need to get in the other lane. Use the headlights for guidance to make out the street corner and turn." Torrey's forced laugh sent Holt's stomach plummeting downward. At least his anatomy righted. Whatever came next, he didn't want any distractions from his innards deciding to let their protests spew forth.

Since they turned onto Main, no traffic had passed them. In fact, they hadn't seen a car in the last hour. Holt put on his turn signal to be safe. He pulled into the other lane, hoped his or Torrey's would-be guardians kept the road clear and the way open for the turn he needed to make.

As if on cue, lightning flashed not once, but twice. The corner came into sight and disappeared just as quick. Holt inched by the car stranded close to the curb by mere feet, thanks to the heavenly burst. He wasn't an overly religious man, but tonight he didn't think twice about mouthing a quiet thank you and keep it up as he drove on.

Torrey's pent up sigh rushed out. "Talk about freaky!"

Holt gripped the steering wheel tighter. He willed himself to keep his focus on driving and not glancing at Torrey. "For sure. We're almost at the edge of City Centre. Keep an eye out for when we get closer to the store."

Silence mixed with the tension-filled air around them. Holt knew better than to attempt small talk. He needed to focus on his driving, not letting his imagination ramp-up his apprehensions. Still he reached over and patted Torrey's arm. Her hand momentarily covered his and squeezed. Some reassurance was better than none. He blinked and squinted against the blur his watering eyes presented. *Come on contacts don't fail me now.* Torrey's sudden gasp got his attention. "What's wrong?" Holt pumped the brakes to avoid skidding.

"We went past the store. The lights are out." Torrey's muttered curse reached his ear.

"Is that a big problem? I know many businesses leave them on for security." Holt eased the car back into the lane. He watched for a place to turn around.

Torrey's shuddered sigh didn't sound great nor did her rustling. "I'm less worried about security. This storm is more than any burglar would want to venture out in. It's finding the road to my place. I use the street lights to mark the way."

Holt took two short breaths as he reminded himself to not chuckle. Torrey's multitasking as she drove left no room for distractions. Thank god, her Bluetooth didn't work in his car. Or she'd be preoccupied with other things rather than them. After his first two rides with her driving, he'd asked her to turn off the offending headset and cell phone until they arrived where they were going. Once she understood his preference for her focusing on him and her driving, she'd made sure they had few interruptions.

"I'm sure we'll see the street signs." Holt flicked on the car's high beam lights. No other cars had passed in the last twenty minutes. He hoped they could get out of the storm soon. He didn't like the way water kept splashing up on the windshield as he drove. That indicated more pooling and ponding water on already-slippery road surfaces. Not good, even in calmer rainstorms. This wind-driven one would make driving impossible within a short amount of time.

"Thanks, Holt." Torrey leaned forward. Holt shot a quick glance at her. He knew she wanted to get out of the storm, too. She'd chafed her arms several times since they'd gotten in the car. Cold summer storms weren't fun. Chilling from one could lead to a cold. He hated being sick. He knew Torrey did, too.

Torrey tapped on the windshield. "I see the turn. About forty more feet and you want to ease into the parking lot. Go back until you see the exit sign for Myers Way." Holt gripped the wheel, focusing on the narrow beams of light in front of him. The glare from the slick pavement and the rain sluicing down the windshield made seeing very difficult. "Once I get to Myers, which way? I need to focus on getting us there."

"Turn left when you see the lawnmower place. We'll pass several businesses before we get to the bridge over Mill Creek. I know it will be crossable." Torrey hunched forward in her seat, wiping at the condensation accumulating on the windows.

Holt worked his way past the dark edge of the building. He saw the sign for Myers as he slowed. "The cop said Old Mill Creek Road was underwater. How do you know Mill Creek isn't flooding?"

Torrey turned to him. Lightning flashed, illuminating the interior of the car. Her megawatt smiled plunged deep into his chest. Last time she'd smiled like that at him, he'd wined, dined, and satisfied her to the point where he almost asked her to consider something more serious between them. Before he'd gotten up the nerve to ask her three weeks later, she was gone. This time, he wasn't screwing up.

"I'm on the redistricting committee. The re-grade to the creek bed finished last week. We also had the bridge reinforced now that the city voted for expanding Dry Creek Estates." Torrey's tone eased Holt's apprehension. He hoped they didn't have to go much farther.

Ten more minutes of palm-sweating driving found them at the edge of the wooden bridge. Holt stopped. Mud spattered the windshield and windows. They bounced and straddled through, over and around more puddles and potholes than he ever remembered Myers Way having. Going back wasn't an option. The last puddle they'd drove through had sent streams of dark water across the hood of the car. Holt knew he owed more prayers of thanks to the powers-that-be. The car kept on running. Mud covered headlights wouldn't be bright enough to drive by safely. Neither side of the narrow two lanes provided turn-around-space that wasn't already water covered.

With the high beams on again, he rolled down his window. Leaning out, he waited until his eyes focused. He heard the rushing water before he saw it. He could make out the water swirling angrily below the bridge. His calm exterior hid his internal angst. Getting them across the bridge and onto the higher ground illuminated by the headlights needed priority. Racing over the bridge didn't make sense as the boards looked slick in the reflection from the lights. Holt took a deep breath, rolling up his window. He put the car into gear and started on to the bridge. "Hold on. We're going across."

Torrey opened her window several moments later. Rain slashed inward, pelting her face. "We're almost halfway across. Go ahead. I'll keep watch on this side. The water is rising. We can get over if we go now."

Just as she finished speaking, a bolt of lightning lit up the sky. A loud crackle and sizzle sounded. The hair on the back of her neck and arms stood up. Holt's "Oh shit" rang through the car. Torrey heard the engine race. She grabbed ahold of the overhead handle and prayed.

Holt gunned the motor. It was now or never. He'd seen the exact path of the bolt. A large tree about one hundred yards down the opposite bank groaned and began tumbling toward the bridge. Even reinforced, the old wooden bridge wouldn't withstand the impact. He couldn't back up without being able to see behind him. Darkness prevented that. There was nothing to keep them from plunging into the deep angry waters of Mill Creek when the tree hit. One way out of the tree's path lay before them. Holt reached over with one hand, pulling

Torrey away from the open window. She squirmed, trying to get away, fighting him as he tugged her away from the window. He grasped the steering wheel firmly in his other and floored the gas pedal. Holt cursed, "Damn it, Torrey. Keep still and let me drive."

Holt let go of Torrey as he grabbed the steering wheel with both hands to keep the car from fishtailing. The tires squealed as the car lurched forward.

Chapter Five

Torrey sat upright in her seat. She tightened her hold on the handle above the door with both hands. Prayers she hadn't uttered since her Catholic high school days leapt to her lips. Swallowing hard, she fought to keep from crying out as a loud groan sounded and a tall, thick tree began careening toward them.

Moments flashed behind her closed eyes. When she'd slammed them shut, she didn't know nor did she care. Vivid close-ups of she and Holt ran in succession. The time he'd teased her about the run in her panty hose the first time they met in junior college. Their first passionate kiss that led to them hooking up and realizing the mutual attraction igniting between them. The last one played out slowly. Holt, naked and hard, raked his eyes hotly over her. He licked his lips in anticipation. The lust lighting his eyes reached deep into her belly, working its way into the core of her hormones. As one hand slid up her waist, his other tangled in her hair, pulling her tight against him. Nothing separated them. Not even her shoulder-length hair. Belly to belly, intimately they fitted together. Heat rolled off each of them, engulfing them in snugger swirls as it looped and circled around them.

Holt tugged her hair, easing her head back as he found her neck. Wet nips and nuzzles followed her jaw line. Upward he worked, leaving a trail to what he sought, her parted lips ready to receive his eager kiss.

He left her no opportunity to sigh or do more than quickly catch a breath before his tongue plunged in, seeking hers. Strong and heady like his cologne, his taste rolled over her taste buds, filling her mouth with remnants of the cinnamon mints he loved, bursts of his own essence mingled with hers. Deep inside her, a fire began scalding her with need that refused to go unheeded. Her nipples tightened with hope, awaiting his caress as he loosened his fingers from her hair. Closer they moved toward her aching tips. He broke off their kiss as his hand reached her areola. He licked his fingers before reaching for her nipple.

"Torrey," Holt's voice whispered. She licked her lips, thrusting her chest toward him. "Torrey, I need directions. Come on, speak to me. Are you okay?"

Torrey snapped open her eyes. Holt's worried gaze greeted her. They made it? Gotten across the bridge?

"Directions?" Torrey cringed at the squeakiness of her voice. She sounded like she'd taken a toke of helium. Clearing her throat, she tried speaking again. "Sorry, I'm here. I think my sanity is out there, quivering with disbelief."

Holt's hand covered hers. His warm hand felt wonderful against her cold ones. Lord, when had that happened?

Holt took her hand between his and chafed them. "I agree with your sanity. But we're here on the other side. I hear water rushing behind us. Let's get out of here before we end up with gators nibbling our asses."

Torrey's giggles reminded Holt to breathe. He'd held his breath from the moment he'd gunned the car forward. He wanted to wrap his arms around her and kiss her. They'd spurned death for a few moments, but if they didn't move soon, they'd be fighting for their lives again.

"I'm heading up the road. You tell me when we're near where we need to be. I want nothing more to do with this cold rain tonight. The sooner we're safe, the better." Holt brought Torrey's hand to his lips. He brushed his tongue over her knuckles. Her small jerks and gasp told him she was with him. As much as he hated to burst the bubble he'd created, he needed to get them to higher ground. "Hold on! I'm gunning it again."

Five hundred feet up the road, Holt began breathing easier. The houses around them had electricity. He turned onto a side street and parked. Torrey hadn't said a word after he'd raced up the incline and down the other side of the small hill. He heard her movements as she closed her window and rustled in her seat. He needed directions. If they needed to evacuate further, some idea of where they were was better than none. Holt unclicked his seatbelt and turned cattycornered in his seat, facing Torrey. "Take a deep breath, and let it out."

He couldn't see much even with the porch lights and the few streetlights nearby. One...two...three...Did he go for the full five count he used with his meditation exercises or reach for her now? Deciding touch made the best sense, Holt extended his hand.

Torrey wrapped her arms tighter around herself. Pulling her drenched sweater around her wouldn't help the chills rapidly working their way up and down her arms. Streams of water ran down her cheeks, ending in drips off her jaw and chin onto her soaking-wet top and sweater. She needed to answer Holt. Could she utter a single word? If she took her tongue from between her teeth, would they chatter as hard as her shivers shook her?

Warmth coiled around her wrist, snapping her attention outward. Torrey blinked, knowing her scream stayed trapped in her dry, hurting throat. She couldn't flinch. Movement felt like a slow-motion movie. At least she could face Holt with some stilted effort and get his attention.

"I know you're tired." Holt's welcome voice soothed her. "I can feel you're cold. You need to tell me where we are."

Pulling her hand free from under the arm he held, Torrey raised her trembling fingers to her mouth. She traced her lips, rubbing her fingers harder against them on the second pass. Twinges of pain rolled over them and into her jaw. Good she wasn't numb. Slowly she inserted two fingers gingerly into her parted lips. Moving her lips back and forth and puckering around her fingers, Torrey brushed her tongue against them. Drops of saliva coated them as she raked the bottom of her tongue over them. Maybe she could get a word or two out.

Taking her hand away from her mouth, she licked her lips. "I–I think we're in North S–S–Side." Praise be, she could speak.

"Okay. How far from your place are we?" Torrey squinted, trying to make out Holt's face. She wanted to close her eyes. *Sleep*...how delicious that word sounded. Who said it? The word echoed like a drumbeat inside her. Yawning, she tried to shake her head, working some sense into her befuddled thoughts.

Holt knew better than to grab Torrey. His volunteer work with the local EMTs and Gwen's agency taught him the basics of dealing with a person in shock. Torrey shook more with each passing moment. Hypothermia was next if he didn't get her out of those wet clothes soon. "Slow is okay. Is your place close by? One word answers will do."

"Ye–yes. T–two streets over." Good, she could answer him. Her stammers indicated her internal temperature dropped more than he figured.

"Street name?" Holt hoped she could get it out. He knew from talking with Gwen that Torrey lived in one of the newest combined townhome and single-family sections of Cascade Bay.

The rest of Torrey's response slurred beyond comprehension. Holt hoped he could figure it out. "Simon something?" he asked.

Torrey's rapid nods and hissing said he'd guessed right. "I'll look for a street sign with Simon on it. If you see it before me, rap on your window to get my attention."

Holt started the car and threw the heater on high. He didn't care if the windows fogged up. He would drive with his window open if he had to. Keeping Torrey coherent and awake mattered. If she started to fade on him, he'd cut the heat back.

Twenty minutes later, a loud rap caught his attention. How many street signs had he gawked at and tried to read, he didn't know. Two streets over he'd given up reading them clearly. Hope kept him going that Torrey would signal they were close.

"T–T–Turn h–h–ere," Torrey stuttered.

Holt turned onto the street to his left. He passed two sections of single-family homes. Another rap sounded. Holt eased the car to a stop. Torrey pointed across the street from where they sat. "Th–There. Left o-one." she stammered.

Holt made out the driveway between the two townhouses. He pulled in, letting go of the pent-up breath he held. She had a garage. Inside was the best place to park his car. Or was it?

"Torrey," Holt began. He reached for her, knowing her tired, cold state messed up her thought process. Cupping her cheek, he urged her to look at him. "Is your car in the garage?"

"Yes, st–t–op–p."

Holt nodded his understanding. "The opener?"

Torrey held up her purse. Her hand shook as she tried to reach inside. Holt reached across and covered her hand with his.

"Let me." Holt worked his fingers between Torrey's chilled fingers. "Let go," he whispered. Slowly easing her hand off her purse strap, Holt kept his eyes on her.

Holt locked eyes with Torrey. Her glassy-eyed look worried him. How much more could she endure without reaching a critical point? Hell, his hands felt warm compared to hers, and he knew his were starting to numb from the cold rain. The car's heater helped some. Driving with partially open windows sucked most of the warmth out as they moved. Sitting still aided in keeping the temperature from dipping. It did nothing for the cold, wet, clammy clothes they wore.

Holt fumbled as he unzipped Torrey's purse. He needed to look down. Torrey needed care. Keeping her safe mattered. *Why?* his conscience asked.

Why did this matter? The sinking feeling he got in the pit of his gut every time she shivered said why. Shaking his head, he glanced down.

He worked the zipper open with his other hand. A small square box started to fall out. Holt trapped it against the purse.

"Is this it?" He held up his hand, his palm toward Torrey. Holt caught her nod as he looked up.

He pushed the largest button on the opener. The garage door began creeping up. Lights flickered on inside.

Holt squeezed Torrey's hand as it dropped from her, combing her hand through her hair. "We're safe. Let me pull in and get us out of this storm."

Torrey's murmur escaped him as another bolt of lightning split the sky and thunder boomed in reply.

Holt eased his car in beside hers. She still had her red Miata convertible. He bet the odometer read over one hundred thousand miles. He remembered her pride and joy driving down the Coast Highway to Big Sur with the top down. The wind blowing over them as the sun baked their skin. That was another time and place. He swallowed hard, pulling his lips tight against each other, as a surge of joy bubbled in his gut. If Torrey had driven tonight, he might not be where he was. Fate might be listening to his silent prayers after all.

Holt pushed the large button again. The garage door began closing. Opening his door, he turned the ignition off. Torrey's heavy sigh cut through him worse than the last clap of thunder and lightning had. He knew that sigh all too well. He'd given a few of his own after a long week in court. Drained and ready to collapse where they sat would do neither of them any good. Time wasn't their friend any longer. Reality set in quickly as the interior of the car cooled. "Come on. We both need to shuck these damn wet clothes. I'll get my gym bag out of the trunk. You gonna be all right to get your door unlocked?"

Torrey's slow nod and jumbled moves told him more than if she'd spoken. He knew from working with trauma victims they worked on autopilot, doing what was necessary. She needed help. Was her blasted pride keeping her from asking?

Holt unlocked the trunk as he moved around the car. He reached in and grabbed the strap of his gym bag, slinging it over his shoulder. At least he had dry clothes to change into. Getting Torrey inside came next.

Ten minutes later, he dropped his bag on the kitchen floor. Torrey sat slumped in a nearby chair. Her purse lay on the table. Pools of water formed under her as water ran down her arms and legs. She was soaked more than she let on. Crap! So much for her getting undressed on her own.

"Torrey, come on. Stand up for me." Holt took ahold of Torrey's arm and tugged. Her blank face turned toward him. Her partially closed lids indicated she was probably half-asleep. Great, undressing a semi coherent woman wouldn't be easy. Leaning her back in the chair, Holt assessed his options. He could strip both of them down in the kitchen and worry about the wet floor and clothes later. Or he could find her bedroom or bathroom, get his damp clothes off, and come back for her. Neither worked, given how limp Torrey appeared.

Another idea flashed as he pulled his polo shirt over his head. He grabbed his gym bag and tossed it on the table. His oversized sweatshirt would keep Torrey warm long enough to carry her upstairs once he got her shorts and top off. As he rummaged in the bag, another thought came to mind. He'd looked at buying in the complex during initial construction stages. Shit, these places had bedrooms on main floor as well as upstairs. Last time he'd been at her place, she lived in a rented condo. He didn't have time to play hide-and-seek looking for her bedroom.

"Torrey, talk to me, darlin'. Your bedroom is where?" Holt got his answer as her arm rose, fingers pointing away from the staircase. A noisy yawn followed by her rocking forward.

"I sh–show you," Torrey stuttered. As she rose, she flailed her arms trying to remain upright. Holt rushed behind her. Slipping his arm around her waist, he steadied her.

"Stay still, please. I'll get us there. You point the way." Holt's husky voice oozed down her neck, leaving warm spots she thought she'd never feel again. Heat from him filtered through her chilled damp clothes. As his arms settled firmly around her waist, Torrey leaned into him. She swore her teeth would never stop chattering.

"Take steps in the direction you need me to go. I've got you, sweetie." Holt's voice and warmth enveloped her like a huge down quilt. Parts of her wanted to argue. All she could think about was sleep. She moved toward the hall, not sure she could have done it without him.

Holt halted near the door to her laundry room off the main bathroom. "These wet clothes are coming off." He reached for her sweater.

"No–o," Torrey protested. She tried to pull away.

Chapter Six

Holt eased his way around Torrey. He knew she didn't want him undressing her. The sooner he got the wet clothes off her, the better. Hell, he even chilled seeing how soaked her sweater and tank top were. As his gazed roved lower, he noticed the large wet spot between her legs. He tried to swallow and say words. Instead, his throat constricted as he looked up.

Torrey stood before him with her top pulled halfway up over her breasts. Who said a white lace demi bra couldn't be sexy? Her pink, tight nipples pressed against the thin under layer of each cup. Did she wear matching panties?

Holt slowly worked his hand down the buttonhole side of the sweater. Getting her out of it was going to be a challenge if she kept twisting around and bunching her top up. Grabbing her hand, he spun her around until her back was to him. "Stand still. I've seen what you got. Believe me, I don't take advantage of incapable women."

Torrey slurred some response and shook her arm at him. Holt used the movement to distract her while he slid one sleeve down her arm. Moments later, her top, and sweater lay in the washer. "Stay put. I'll get us towels."

Holt moved into the large bathroom. In the mirror, he could see a robe hanging on back of the door. He snatched two of the folded towels from the counter. Maybe Torrey would stop fighting him if he offered her cover. He raced down the hall. As he turned to where he left Torrey standing, he hesitated.

Torrey stood before him in all her natural glory. She'd managed to get her shorts and shoes off without falling down. Her panties bunched around her ankles like a pile of snow. One breast hung below her bra and the other, still covered by the cup, looked as though it wanted release. Tossing her robe over his shoulder, Holt shook out a towel. "Here, I think this will help."

Torrey looked up, blinked at him, and pitched forward.

Holt rushed forward, tossing the towel aside as he moved. Two more steps and he would have her. Thrusting one arm out, Holt worked himself between Torrey and the doorjamb she fell toward. He went rigid, bracing to catch her.

"Uhhh," he groaned as Torrey landed against him. His free arm slid around her, hoping to steady both of them. Flesh brushed against his open palm, filling his hand. He cupped the flesh without thought and pulled Torrey firmly against him.

A yowl sounded behind him followed by growls and yips. Shit, he'd forgotten her blasted menagerie. A quick glance over his shoulder revealed the motley trio, two mutts, and a mouthy Siamese cat. Mutts didn't fit the two dachshunds. Three rescue animals and a cold, wet, partially naked Torrey in his arms. Holt rolled his eyes, shook his head, and bent down. When this was over, Stuart owed him big time. Maybe he didn't, his quirky conscience teased.

Picking Torrey up in his arms, Holt shot the motely trio a dirty look. "Hush," he hissed, moving around them and into the short hall he hoped led to Torrey's bedroom.

His intuition paid off. The last door off the hall revealed a large master bedroom. He laid Torrey down as gently as he could. Her bra remained transfixed across her breasts. One strap lay partway down her arm while the other stayed on her shoulder. Holt reached up for her robe. Nothing. The robe must have fallen as he picked her up or—a quick look revealed where it lay. Bunched between her legs, a dark mauve color drew his gaze.

Holt reached for the robe. His fingers grazed her flesh close to her mons. Heat surged inside him. Deep in his groin, a small flame flickered, gasping for fuel to grow. His throat constricted as guilt flooded him at the same time. Need mixed with desire, threatening to exceed what common sense he had left. How long had they been on the road? How much time had passed since he realized they needed dry clothes and sleep?

Sleep? Where had that come from? Holt bit his lip and worked his hand away from the mound of hair and flesh it touched. Torrey needed help. Sex could wait. He couldn't take his eyes of her as her chest rose and fell as she breathed. Good, at least he'd gotten her past the shivers stage. He pulled the robe from between her legs. Shaking it out, he inhaled.

Bits of her favorite perfume tantalized his nose and disappeared. Memories endangered him from keeping focused. He draped the robe over her. For extra warmth, he tossed part of the quilt spread over her feet. One last look told him she probably slept. Good thing. He needed to get out of his wet clothes.

As Holt moved back into the hall, yowls and sharp barks met him. Three sets of glowing eyes watched him. Poor things needed reassurance, too. He didn't have it in him to fuss at them like they possibly needed. Best he could manage was to see if they needed water and food. That had to wait until he knew Torrey was going to be all right.

Holt halted near the bathroom, shielding his eyes from the bright overhead light he had left on in there. He saw the large soaker tub as he reached into turn off the light. This would do it. Warm water and soap followed by sleep would help. Holt stumbled across the tile floor. Yawn after yawn menaced him as he filled the tub. How long could he hold out before exhaustion claimed him? The bolts of adrenaline were wearing off.

Holt turned the water off. Shivers ran down his back and over his chest. Lord, even the heat from the overhead fan chilled him. He needed to get Torrey in here. Having both of them warm and dry mattered.

Holt cussed as he fumbled with his belt. His hands felt like they belonged to someone else. His fingers refused to cooperate and ease his belt open, much less the zipper of his jeans. Several curses later, Holt pushed his wet jeans and boxers down his legs. He hopped on one leg, pulling the wet mess off his foot. He stumbled, catching the edge of the sink, before he freed his other foot. He tossed the cold, wet items in a pile near the bathroom door. He turned, ready to go get Torrey. In the medicine cabinet mirror, his reflection gazed back at him. His hair stood up on end. Dark areas showed beneath his eyes. His five-o'clock shadow stood out. Even the matted hair on his chest seemed to shout out how tired and disheveled he looked. He gave into the childish response running through him. He stuck out his tongue and put his fingers in his ears.

A whimper drew his attention. Holt rushed down the hall. Torrey's moans grew louder. He knew the sound of pain all too well. His stint as a volunteer dispatcher taught him the essence of timing. Torrey needed help warming up and someone to ensure she didn't hurt herself as she did. Holt stood still near the bed. The cat and dachshunds lay on the bed close by her. Every time Torrey thrashed and moaned, the cat's ears flattened back.

Holt slipped one arm under Torrey's legs. He worked the other beneath her head as she turned sideways.

"Torrey, come on, love. Open your eyes. I'm here." Holt squatted as he rolled her into his arms and against him. He rose slowly, not wanting to jostle her or frighten her. He glanced at her as he turned. Her gaze met his. She seemed to be sleepily looking at him. Her unfocused blinks followed by a yawn confirmed his suspicions.

She needed to be more awake before he put her in the tub. Talking to her might work. "I know you're in pain. We'll take care of that in a moment. Can you tell me where it hurts?"

"Huh?"

Holt kissed the top of Torrey's head. She'd answered him. "Where do you hurt?" he repeated.

"Lights. So bright." Torrey's hand shot up, covering her eyes. "Hurt all over." She moaned as he entered the bathroom.

"Just a moment, sweetie." As he maneuvered past the counter with Torrey in his arms, he managed to grab two towels and then draped them loosely on the commode. Holt eased Torrey on to the edge of the tub. He turned her until her feet dipped into the water. He tested the water before he slid her down into it. "This should help."

Torrey's murmurs changed to oohs and ahs. Holt leaned her back against the tub's backrest. Easing his legs over the sides of the tub, Holt sat in the water, pulling Torrey back against him. A short soak, followed by a brisk scrub, should help warm both of them. Now if he could get his cock to behave...

Eight hours later

Torrey sat up, and the sheet covering her pooled around her waist. She blinked as one yawn after another gripped her. Bright sun filtered through the partially opened blinds covering her bedroom window. As she reached to stretch, the hair on her arms stood up. A cool breeze blew over her shoulders and down her chest. She glanced down. She was—when the hell had this—Flashes of the prior night came racing back.

Grasping the sheet, she yanked it up over her bare breasts, tucking it under her arms. Muffled sounds came from beside her. She closed her eyes and said the one novena she remembered. The snoring increased.

Easing back down into the rest of the covers, Torrey willed her conscience to ignore the occupant lying beside her. A large hand slipped out from beneath the blanket covering him. His tousled hair peeked out from under the top edge of the sheet. Was he as naked as she was? Another image flared behind her closed eyes. Torrey swallowed hard. Memories came pouring back in coherent pieces compared to the prior night's disjointedness.

"We didn't...did we?" Her hand covered her mouth as she voiced the main thought demanding an answer, her conscience pinged her again.

"Didn't what?" a sleepy male voice asked.

Torrey closed her eyes, swallowed, and shot another quick prayer heavenward. *Grant me the sense to not read more into this than there is.*

"You know." She shrugged and pulled the sheet tighter around her.

"Stop snitching the covers." Holt sat up, tugging at the sheet. "If I knew, I wouldn't ask."

His sleepy grin and wink sent more ripples through her than she cared to admit. If they had made love...Wait, the love couldn't be there—could it? If they'd fucked...She grimaced at that word, too.

"Why the face?" Holt's voice wrapped around her like a warm, crocheted throw. Torrey gulped and faced him.

"Ah, no particular reason." She tried to grin. Another yawn grabbed her instead. She tried to cover her mouth with her hand, and that was not happening. Instead, Holt's hand snaked out from under the blankets and caught hers.

"Something has you upset. Spill it." He raised her hand to his mouth and ran his tongue over her knuckles.

Chapter Seven

Torrey tried to tug her hand free from Holt's, wanting to get away from the streaks of desire racing up her arm and plunging deep into her. She'd been doing great with keeping things cool and aloof with the men she dated. Recently, a couple of them had her waking up at night hot and bothered by her wet dreams. There was no other description for it. Her swollen clit and dewy nether lips said it all. Okay, so she'd masturbated, worn out a cheap vibrator, and ordered a new one. She hadn't broken her cardinal rule of no sex until she connected with the guy on a deeper level.

"Come on. Tell me what has you wrought up?" Holt turned her hand over, inching his lips along her palm, nipping, and nibbling as he could.

Torrey shook her head, tugged harder, and frowned. "You could let go of my hand." There, she'd said it. From the look she got, Holt wasn't about to acquiesce.

"No, I like what I'm doing. You got a complaint?" His cheesy grin and the slow shake of his head set off more smoke in her lower half. He was flirting, right? Messing with her head? He had to be.

"Uh-mm." She couldn't get more words out. Holt's other hand cupped the underside of her breast. His thumb traced the space just below her nipple in a back and forth motion. Did her nipples have to respond? Even the left-out one pouted in response to the one getting attention.

"Oh, my—" Torrey began, only to stop as Holt sucked her fingers one by one into his mouth.

Torrey squirmed. Her clit throbbed every time Holt drew her finger into his mouth. What was it with her? She inhaled, blinked, exhaled, and shrugged her shoulders. Wrong move. Her breast settled into Holt's hand as if he remembered how she liked her breasts fondled. As if her nipples had a mind of their own, they pouted more, begging for hands-on caresses from him.

Holt drew Torrey's middle and index finger between his lips and licked their underside along their tips and over the top. He noticed her squirm as he suckled harder on the downward stroke back toward her knuckles. He knew he had her turned on. Her breasts swelled, and her nipples stood out against the sheet. He wanted more than a quick orgasm. Could she handle more? Would she listen to what he had to say?

"Torrey," he whispered, moving closer. "Why are you worried? We know each other. Seen each other naked, even bathed together like last night. Delicious as always, too."

"Holt," Torrey began, her words slurred as he leaned closer. "I–I'm not su–re you get it."

"Get what?" he asked, nipping her shoulder. Holt could feel the coarse and needy desire flowing off her. He bet if he inhaled deeply, he could smell her pheromones.

Torrey's shuddered exhale drew his attention back out of himself and to them. Holt wanted the connection to be more than the physical chemistry that sizzled between them. Lovemaking took two, two people making love with each other and not to someone for their own selfish release. Orgasms were grand and the release well worth the effort and work. However, finesse and tact helped add much more to things. Fucking could be fun and friendly. Warm and cozy with the right person, too. He'd shared that repeatedly with Torrey. What had brought him to the realization he wanted and needed more? He still wasn't sure. The night they'd spent hours talking and mixing tantric sex with their conversation stuck out in his mind. Both of them revealed how much their friendship meant to them and how deep their affection ran. Neither of them had quite said the L word.

Right now, he sensed Torrey's resistance. Her stiffness of words and body language practically screamed out her turmoil. Holt wanted to hear her out if she'd talk. The pregnant silence between them had to go. Torrey needed to know he wanted to hear what was going on. The old Holt would have pushed on with sex. Not this Holt. He wanted her to see and know how he'd changed.

"I didn't get what?" he repeated, putting his arm around Torrey's shoulder. "I don't remember you being this upset last night. Or ever in our friendship. Talk to me, please."

As his hand reached her other shoulder, he exerted a bit of pressure. She needed to let go of her dam of control. If Torrey would open up some, their communication might flow better and easier. She knew she could trust him, didn't she?

Torrey wiped her sweaty palms down the sheet, stopping close to her breasts. Holt's touch affected her like before. None of their chemistry had vanished. Still, she needed to know what happened last night. Had she acted on impulse or held true to her standards? What good were standards when the one person she connected with on other levels sat next to her, her conscience chided. "Gee, thanks, conscience," she muttered aloud.

"Me? Your conscience?" Holt's snort broke her train of thought.

"Sorry," she offered, trying to shrug and keep the sheet in place. "Caught up in my thoughts."

Holt's smile and wink caught her off guard. She tried swallowing and working her throat to voice a reply. No luck. His touch and nearness cut off words and coherent thoughts. Part of her wanted to just feel and enjoy. Was feeling and enjoying awful?

"I think you're worried. Maybe about last night?" Holt knew he took a chance saying that aloud. He glanced at Torrey. She seemed preoccupied with the damn sheet again. Enough already. Holt reached out with his free hand and pulled.

"What the—what are you—crap!" Torrey's words flowed faster than her hands moved. Holt kept pulling slowly as the sheet fell, revealing her luxuriant breasts. With the hand on her opposite shoulder, he pushed more, hoping to get her off-balance. Once she was against him and exposed, she'd stopped this nonsense of prim and proper. One more push and...

"Holt," Torrey gasped. Part of him wanted to shout "pay dirt." That sounded like the old Holt. Not that he entirely left. He'd gotten some couth and learned to keep his mouth shut when appropriate. He'd learned control as he studied to pass his bar exam. Concentration and studying while he worked taught him a lot about patience and fulfillment. If anyone said law school was easy, he'd laugh until his sides hurt. The accelerated program had almost done him in. Determination paid off and got him where he wanted to be. Now he would use the same in snagging Torrey.

"Stop fidgeting. Unless you want something different." Holt leaned back against the quilted headboard and his pillows, taking Torrey with him. He eased her up on him, nestling her beside him, touching, and without the sheet covering her. With it bunched at their waists, both their chests were exposed. He itched to take her nipples between his thumb and finger, rolling them as he remembered her liking. Good thing his aching hard-on hid beneath the sheet and blanket covering him.

"What makes you think I want anything?" Torrey's exasperated tone iced down his chest, wilting his cock some. Time to thaw her cold resolve.

Holt cupped Torrey's cheek. "This is why." He leaned in, brushed his lips over hers. He didn't move away. He went back for more. His tongue traced her bottom lip before he caught it between his teeth, worrying it slightly.

Torrey's hands fell on his chest, her nails scratching lightly as they worked their way down him. Holt pressed his lips more fully on hers. Her tongue met his as he retraced her upper lip. A small taste of her minty toothpaste lingered on her. Would she let him in if he asked?

Holt opened his mouth, deepening the kiss. With each swipe of his tongue, he explored Torrey's response. She met him and didn't withdraw.

Bolts of wanton need washed over Torrey as her palms flattened on Holt's chest. Hot male flesh scalded her fingers. She didn't care. The burn felt fantastic. The few dates she'd tried with men she related with cerebrally lacked the attraction and catalytic ignition she looked for. Sex felt different with Holt. The depth and level had rocked her every time they'd come together. This time she burned and didn't want to stop. Had she found the complete link she wanted?

"Holt, I want..." The rest of her words went unspoken. He took the cue and slipped inside her mouth. Their tongues met in a passionate duel. Her cinnamon mouthwash raced over her taste buds. Flashes of him using it last night as they brushed their teeth came back. Torrey attempted to inhale. Musky male scent filled her nostrils. Not unwashed sweatiness. Instead, almond soap and natural male pheromones teased her.

Strong male hands eased their way over her taut shoulders, rubbing and lingering on the knots in places she'd forgotten about. How long had it been since someone cared about her? Gave TLC without asking for anything in return? Holt gave and was giving whether he realized it or not. When had he changed? Why?

"Not giving a penny or fig about your thoughts unless they're on me." Holt's husky whisper warmed her neck and face. She'd forgotten he'd broken off the kiss as he touched the hard muscles along her shoulder blades. Behind her closed eyes, she gave in to enjoying the caring warmth pulsing through her with each stroke. The strength in his caress spoke of his confidence, and at the same time, his gentleness as he rubbed back over the loosened muscles told of his care and concern. Lord, the man's hands felt like manna to her. He could keep the massage aspect up all day. Torrey blissfully sighed.

"That is sheer nirvana."

Holt's "good" rumbled his chest and vibrated hers as well. Torrey inhaled, knowing every breath she took brought her more in touch with Holt. She eased her hands from between them, enjoying every moan and "hmm" Holt made as she did. With her hands free, she opened her eyes. His deep-blue eyes met hers. She didn't need to look further to know he smiled inside and out. Their glow told of his joy and pleasure. She gave into her emotions and touched him like she'd wanted to since he de-sheeted her.

Cupping Holt's cheek, she blew him a kiss. Licking her lips, she voiced the annoying question that refused to stay quiet. "Did we fuck last night?"

Holt rocked back, pulling away from her. *"Did we what?"*

Chapter Eight

Holt's frown sent ripples of anxiety deep into her gut. Torrey gulped, moving away, hoping the additional distance would ease the rapid tension she sensed building between them. "Fuck. As in have sex. I'm sure you understand the word and actions."

Previously the word never fazed Holt. His continued scowl and stare cooled her more than if he'd cussed or said anything. He had changed. Sure, he talked about it some as they ate. Even made suggestions about how he did things differently. This silent treatment cut deep. Would a simple "I'm sorry" suffice? Torrey dropped her hands to her lap. She toyed with the edge of the sheet before she looked up.

"Holt, I'm sorry." She gazed at him. His frown softened. His shoulders didn't. Okay, the apology only went so far. "I get the feeling you need to say something."

Holt nodded. He took a couple of breaths. How long did he make her wait? Squirming and wondering would do her good. Hurting her intentionally wasn't an option. Last night was wonderful, holding her and taking care of her.

"Torrey, I don't fuck." Holt held up his hand, fending off her attempt to speak. "I don't fuck people I care about."

Torrey's silence dampened his ire. He wanted to roll her over and bury himself balls-deep in her until she cried out in pleasure. That wouldn't work. That amounted to fucking. Taking another deep breath, Holt held it. He let out a heavy sigh and took Torrey's hand.

"Torrey, last night neither of us was sure what the next moment would bring." Holt caught her chin, tipping her head back and meeting her eyes. "I want to be sure you understand why I did what I did last night."

Torrey didn't break eye contact with him. Her brief nod told him she wanted to hear what he had to say. Holt let go of Torrey's chin. He faced her. His legs touched hers. She didn't flinch or pull away. Good. She worried about a sexual interlude between them. Why, he didn't understand. That remained for a different discussion.

"Go on," Torrey said. Holt noted her quieter tone. He wanted to reach out and reassure her. Her need for reassurance touched him deeper than he expected. His heart skipped a beat when she licked her lips and glanced away. Lord, he hadn't realized how much she'd gotten under his skin again. He didn't care that she had. He wanted her to accept they were here because they wanted to be. Maybe needed to be.

"To say nothing happened last night is not completely true. Something did happen. I'm not sure if you're ready to hear what did happen." Holt paused, his eyes on her face watching for any clue. Would she offer her version of what went on?

"Should I tell you what I think happened?" Torrey's question caught him off guard.

"I–I...You remember last night?" Holt closed his eyes, counted to three, and opened them. He looked Torrey in the eye, waited for her to answer him.

"Yes. Well—er—not all. Bits and pieces." Her shrug told him she wanted to be sure what had gone down.

Holt touched Torrey's wrist. He slowly slid his fingers down across her palm, not stopping until he interlaced his fingers with hers. "Let me reassure you nothing happened that you need to be worried or ashamed about. I—"

Torrey held up her hand. "Stop. Okay?"

Holt nodded. Torrey inhaled and let go the pent-up angst she'd been holding in. Wetting her lips, she decided which of the jumbled pieces of her fragmented memories from the prior evening she wanted to get out first.

"I remember crossing the bridge and the drive to find my place. I can vaguely put together getting inside." Torrey glanced at the clock on her dresser. "I didn't realize it's after ten."

"Your point is?" Holt turned until he could see the clock on her dresser behind him. "It's daylight." He pointed to the window.

"No kidding. This window faces east. The sun is brighter through it until noon. That tells me there's clouds or a storm." Torrey flung back the covers. She glanced down, felt heat begin to build along her neck, and put a hand to her face. Warm! Christ, was she blushing?

"Instead of giving me more reason to change the subject, you might want to get back in here." Holt patted the bed, holding up the covers she'd easily tossed off.

"It's nothing you ain't seen before." Torrey turned and walked away. Halfway across the room, she stumbled. Walking regally away from Holt wasn't happening. "Damn."

Holt bolted out of the bed. He reached Torrey as she grabbed her foot. "You okay?" He wrapped an arm around her waist, steadying her. "What happened?"

"Mischa's bone!" Torrey pointed to a small round object not far from her other foot. "Doxie hides them under the bed. Mischa leaves them lying out. Like a blasted obstacle course at times."

Several muffled barks sounded. Holt and Torrey turned back toward the bed. As if on cue, two heads popped out from under the bed. Their tongues hung out.

Holt moved closer to Torrey. Chuckling, he kissed the top of her head. "Good thing to know. Those two are accounted for. I remember a cat."

A yowl sounded from behind them. Torrey pointed at Mischa and Doxie. "Siam is probably in the closet. And knowing those two, they chased him in there."

Holt sighed and shook his head. "I'll let him out. You sit down." He guided Torrey back to the bed, making sure she was seated before making his way to the closet. He no more than opened the closet and a grayish-white streak shot out. The dachshunds followed in hot pursuit.

"Great! Do we need to break that up?" He pointed at the open bedroom door. Yowls and barks echoed down the short hall.

"Not unless it gets louder. Or they chase Siam back in here. That is unlikely as he loves to perch on top of the refrigerator and glare down at them." Torrey rubbed her sore foot. "We're good for another half hour."

Holt made his way back to the bed. "Then scoot over."

Torrey shook her head. "I'm not getting back in until I've got answers."

Holt leaned forward until his face was level with hers. He placed his palms flat on the mattress. "You want answers? Here ya go."

Torrey sucked in air. She started to bring up her hands. Holt's next words stopped her.

"We bathed together. Fell into bed and cuddled." Holt's heavy breath blew her bangs out of her field of vision. "Now are you satisfied?"

Torrey swallowed hard. Her throat constricted on her next swallow. Holt's hard-edged tone ripped over her like a dull pair of scissors. She'd pushed him to this. Slowly she raised her hand. She touched his chest. The rapid beat of his heart pulsed beneath her palm. Every breath he took rippled his warm firm muscles across the same area. Torrey looked up and met his gaze.

"Thanks for saying that. I know I can be a pain. I just—" Holt's lips captured hers. His tongue chased hers deep into her mouth. His eyes closed. Torrey inhaled and pressed her lips tighter to his.

Holt peeked through his lashes. Torrey's flushed cheeks echoed his own internal heat. They needed this time together. Now that she knew what had happened last night, would she let him go further? Let him ease her down on the bed with the passion and need they both felt. Time wasn't on their side, but neither did he intend to rush things. He remembered the dry food he found in the cabinet near the refrigerator on one of his forays to the bathroom after he'd slept for a while. The animals would be all right for a while longer thanks to him putting some in a couple of their bowls.

Holt leaned closer, putting more of his weight into his hands without pushing Torrey. He wanted her to follow him of her own accord, not because she felt pressured.

"Holt," Torrey murmured as she broke off the kiss.

"Hmmm, yes?" He wanted more.

Torrey's hands slid up his arms. "Are we going to do something now?" She looped her arms around Holt's neck.

"Could be?" he offered, nipping her neck. "We aren't gonna fuck. Make sure you know that."

Holt's hot breath scalded her ear. She tilted her head to the side, exposing more of her neck. His lips followed, licking and nibbling along her jawline before he captured her earlobe with his teeth.

Torrey moaned deep in her throat. Holt remembered how sensitive her ears were. How the sensual play got her hotter, hornier, and wetter with each suck and nibble. "We're not fucking," she managed to get out in between quick breaths. "What are we doing, then?"

Holt raised his head. His gaze never left hers. His next words broke through the ice she'd incased her heart in. "Making love, darling. Making love."

In the back of her mind, bells and whistles sounded. Her libido held up a sign with *ignore* written in bold letters. She couldn't look away if she wanted to. His glow poured out of him and enveloped her in a huge hug.

Torrey tried breathing deeper. Each breath brought her within inches of her breasts touching his chest. Holt leaned down, angling his head. The closer he got, the warmer Torrey grew. Desire swamped her without regard to anything else.

Holt knew his plan would work. Neither of them could resist the pull of sexual chemistry between them once they acknowledged the magnetism. Long ago, both of them agreed they didn't need barriers from each other. Their mutual respect and friendship kept them safe. Would that work now? Torrey hadn't questioned him on his choice of words. He'd leave well enough alone for now before he voiced what he wanted now that they were together again. Getting her to listen would be another thing.

The closer he got, the further Torrey leaned back. Good, soon she'd fall back or have to lie down. Not that rubbing his pecs against her firm nipples would be bad.

"Sweetums," he whispered, inches from Torrey's delicious mouth. "Why don't you lay back on the bed and get comfortable?"

Torrey's brief nod and "uh-huh" ignited a flame he couldn't put out if he'd tried. What had turned her away from questioning him? *She wants you*, his ego boasted. *Shut up*, his conscience blathered back.

Holt lifted his left arm and began straightening up. Torrey licked her lips as he pulled his right arm away. If his cock got any harder, his balls would knot up. No one else revved up his desire like Torrey. He needed to go at a pace that left both of them fulfilled.

Turning around, Holt backed up against the bed, sitting as he felt the mattress touch the back of his knees. He eased back on his elbows, all the time watching Torrey observe him. The flush on her face grew as her gaze roved over him and down to his groin. He bet if he touched her that scalding hot need would grab him. If she kept up with the eye-humping stares, forget keeping sane. They would be mating like two cats in heat. Not a bad thing. But, he said they were going to make love.

Chapter Nine

Torrey knew that look. Passion rolled off Holt without him doing a thing. His gaze roved over her as if she were water to a drought-stricken man. His eyes lingered where she remembered his favorite parts of her anatomy being.

"Cup your breasts and run your thumbs over your nipples." Holt reached for her.

Torrey licked her lips. His dominant tone rushed over her in ripples until every inch of her pulsed with need. She couldn't submit to any other man the way she did with Holt. His requests contained the hint of edgy desire she enjoyed. He pulled her to the edge until—

"Oh," Torrey moaned. She looked down. Her taut nipple lay between Holt's thumb and forefinger. He plucked and turned his fingers slightly as he worked her nipple like a corkscrew. Each tug sent aching need deep into her. It was as though jagged bolts of lightning scorched their way down to her clit. Every time her nipple throbbed, her clit echoed it.

Torrey leaned on her hand closest to Holt. She brushed her fingers over her sensitized skin between her knee and hip. Goose bumps rose beneath her fingertips. As she reached the top of her thigh, she changed tactics. Using the sharp edge of her manicured nails, she dragged them very lightly over her flesh, murmuring as she came closer to her crotch. "Hmmm, that feels wonderful," she sighed, tossing her head back.

"Are you going to do what I told you to do?" Holt tugged firmer on her nipple. His other hand stroked across her midriff and over her navel, going lower. Would he stop short of her pussy? Tease her until she begged him to finish what he started?

Torrey tried to swallow. Her throat constricted as Holt released her nipple. She inhaled sharply as he puckered his lips. Holt licked his lips. Torrey squirmed. He remembered their subtle signal of his desire, licking his lips repeatedly. The signal he came up with the night he wanted to bring her to crescendo after crescendo of mind-blowing orgasms. He gave as good as he got that night.

"What if I don't want to?" There, tempting fate was worth seeing his reaction. Having him between her legs, licking her until she screamed as one orgasm after another claimed her, made more sense than firing up his dominant side. Of course, he could always tell her no. Then option two might be better. She smiled and stuck out her tongue.

Holt reached over and grabbed Torrey's hand. "I didn't ask if you wanted to. I said do this." He placed her hand palm up on the underside of her breast. He kept his hand beneath hers. "Now put your other hand under your other breast. Be good and you might get a surprise."

Torrey squirmed again. Holt wanted to smile and tease her more. Need pressed him to act rather than verbally spar with her.

"If you want this"—he licked his lips again—"keep cupping, baby. Those nipples are good for nibbling."

Holt leaned forward, toppling Torrey back on the bed. He nuzzled her neck. He nipped along her throat, making his way down to her shoulders. Her moans grew louder as he slid his hand between her legs. Hair as soft as down brushed against his palm. With two of his fingers, he parted her slick pussy lips. He wondered if she tasted as delicious as he remembered her being, sweeter than honey and more of an aphrodisiac than chocolate.

He licked along her collarbone in between nips as she struggled beneath him. The feel of her breasts tight against him as she tried to free her hands turned him on more than he realized. Torrey's warmth and scent filled his nostrils each time he inhaled.

"Holt, let me up, please," Torrey asked. "My hands are going numb."

Holt worried the flesh at the base of her throat one last time. "I understand how that happens. Are you going to behave?" he teased, rising up on his elbow.

Torrey pulled one hand out from between them and then her other. He watched as she opened and closed them before shaking them a few times. She looked up and grinned at him. "What do I get if I behave?"

Holt rolled to his side, taking his hand with him. Taking the two fingers slicked with Torrey's wetness, he glided them in and out of his mouth, licking each with exaggerated motions. "Oh, I don't know."

Torrey yelped as Holt rolled on top of her.

"Shhh. We don't need the trio interrupting us." Holt braced himself on his hands and elevated his chest off hers. Torrey gulped air. The man's cock lay nestled between her legs. Hard and hot never felt this way with anyone else.

Her vibrator would never be the same again. The cold plastic would no longer be her battery-operated relief. Lack of warmth, interaction, and—

"Holt," she cried out. His hips rocked against hers, sending one pulse after another of scorching, wanton need coursing straight to her clit.

Holt's hot breath surged over her neck before his scalding kiss seared her lips as he recaptured hers. Unable to hold back any longer, Torrey parted her lips and sought Holt's tongue with hers. They met at the bridge and dueled. Holt's minty breath mixed with hers. He retreated to her charge, inviting her to follow him. Sweet bursts of mint overwhelmed her taste buds, filled her mouth as she withdrew, hoping he'd give chase.

Holt felt Torrey go slack beneath him. Easing his weight slowly onto her, he lowered his arms keeping a minimum of space between them. He pressed his lips tighter to hers. As he deepened their kiss, he felt her press up against him. Lord, she was wet. Each time his tongue met hers, she squirmed, moving him closer to entering her. Once he slipped inside, there was no going back. No stopping for condoms, not that he worried about catching anything where Torrey was concerned. Once he was balls-deep, he knew she would want him to stay put. The heat rolling off her swallowed his cock and balls and kept reaching higher. Soon the heat's hands would be upon his ass, plunging him deep into her fires. Holt wanted to prolong the burn at a slow pace when that happened.

Torrey's half-swallowed moans and movements inched him to the brink of pushing her legs apart and easing inside. Once joined, rocking together in a slow, uninterrupted pace might help bring them to a simmer as they settled into a more comfortable position.

Torrey's murmurs became incoherent as she pressed tighter to him. She worked her slickness over him. She grabbed one of his hands as she broke off their kiss. "I need your hand here."

She fumbled with placement until he understood. Her sensual nerves needed more stimulation. He cupped her bare breast. Smiling at her gasp, he leaned down, worried her earlobe, and hotly whispered, "Poor baby got left out of the earlier session."

Holt dragged his fingers up the sensitive underside of Torrey's breast. Her gasps and oohs said she liked what he was doing.

Torrey arched her back as Holt captured her pebbled nipple with his fingers. He twisted and tugged as if he worked a well-threaded screw into place.

His callused finger grazed her areola briefly each time he slid his fingers to the bottom of her nipple before returning to its tip. She gulped air as he pulled a bit harder.

"Hmmm, pain can be pleasurable done your way." She smiled at her own quip before looping her arm across Holt's shoulder. "Lord, you are good. Very good at what you do."

Holt's quick grin and slow rock of his hips augmented his throaty "uh-huh."

"I'm ready to slide inside you and soak." Torrey swallowed hard as Holt's husky declaration scorched her throat and ear. Heat dizzily grabbed her and plunged her back into the feeling where coherent thoughts frazzled as quickly as they attempted to cohere. One thought formed in bold black letters behind her semi-closed eyelids. *Protection!*

She knew Holt got tested regularly during his hookup days. That was one of the first discussions either of them had when they decided to act on their mutual attraction. She'd kept up with hers out of habit and concern for her own sexual health. She trusted him, but how much did she trust him? Was she ready to accept him as the one she took the plunge with?

"As much as I love what you're doing." Torrey paused, swallowed, and opened her eyes. "What about—" Her next words were cut off. Holt's cock slipped partially inside her as he slid between her legs.

"Is this what you're wanting?" His question hung between them as if the next pulse of the world waited with them. He didn't move as his eyes met hers. The man knew how badly she wanted him deep within her, bringing her to one rolling orgasm after another. His unabashed words came flowing back as more memories flooded her.

"I love multi-orgasmic women. Lady, I want you there and *soon*." Holt drew out the word soon and dipped his head to hers. "I can't hold out much longer, love. Do you want me to stop?"

Torrey nodded as best she could. A few questions would either keep them going or stop them cold. Holt's sigh cooled her as he pulled back.

She reached down, cupped his ass, and stopped him from pulling out. "Stay put. Please." The look on his face turned from a hard ache to questions. Lord, she could still read him as if they'd never parted. What was it Grandma Getty said about her heart knowing what her mind didn't? Torrey forced her thoughts back to the matter at hand. Having Holt this close and a bit inside her kept more than a slow simmer happening.

His quick nuzzle of her neck and a whispered "go on" turned her on more than she could describe.

"Tests. Yours. When," she managed to get out. "Mine last month. Clean as always." Torrey inhaled deeply. Her chest brushed against Holt's. His molten warmth wormed into her and seared its way deeper into her.

Holt's response warmed her even more. "Mine clean. Last month, too." His quick kiss told her he cared. His concern over her well-being hadn't changed. Still, until she knew if he was going to hang around this time, protection might not be bad.

"Do we want to—you know—" Crap, she'd never been at a loss for words before. Any other time she'd come out and said condoms. Why now? Her heart wanted the bond, the commitment. Her logical mind said actions spoke louder than words.

"Torrey," Holt began, cupping her chin. "If you want condoms, we'll go there. If you want me as I am, we continue."

Torrey caught her lip between her teeth. Holt hadn't moved since she'd asked the question. His gaze stayed fixed on her. Did she take the risk and go back later? Too many questions and too much thinking. Blast her libido. Blast her logical mind.

Holt wished he knew what was going on in Torrey's head. He could see she warred with something. He didn't care if she needed protection or wanted to talk more. His cock would have to wait if things came to that. His swollen balls would have to pout. Pushing aside his need to come would bruise his male ego slightly. Torrey's needs came first. If she was going to trust him, he had to gain that. He had some. He wanted more. He needed her to trust him with her heart. That wouldn't be easy. He hadn't planned to end up here, almost balls-deep in her. Apparently, fate had a different decision waiting for them. If they slowed down, they might be able to regain some control over that outcome.

"Sweetie," Holt sighed. "You make the decision. I'll get the condoms if you need them." He began to slowly pull out of her.

Torrey's hands gripped his hips. "Stop. They're in the nightstand drawer next to us." Holt caught her sideways nod.

Holt grinned and rolled to his side. He stood. Torrey's frown grabbed at his libido. The woman wanted him. *Now* without further waiting, from the way her hands parted her swollen nether lips and stroked her clit. "Easy, babe. I'm rushing."

Holt opened the drawer without taking his eyes off her. He fumbled inside the drawer until his hand met with foil. He glanced down to ensure he held the packet correctly to tear it open. Cool latex met his fingers. A glimpse at Torrey drew his gaze as he dragged the condom over him. One of her hands traced the outline of her slick mons while the other plucked at her swollen nipples. Moments later, he knelt on the bed and guided himself home where he knew pleasure awaited them.

"Yes," Torrey groaned as Holt slid deeper into her. Goodness, it felt wonderful to be so full again. Holt filled her in ways neither her battery-operated boyfriend nor the cold, pulsating plastic did. She smiled as Holt closed his eyes as he set the rhythm of his thrusts. No, not even the heated vibrator the salesperson for one of their regular lines at the store had given her compared to this.

Torrey tightened her muscles on Holt's inward slide. The look on his face pushed her growing temperature higher. As he pulled back, she flexed and worked her muscles along each inch of him.

"Torrey," Holt panted, stopping mid-thrust. "Woman, you've learned a thing or two since we last did this."

"Yes, I have." Torrey clamped down on him and concentrated on working her Kegel muscles. "Let's see what you got to give, handsome."

She spread her legs wider. Inching her hands up Holt's forearms, she bit her lip to keep from crying out as he thrust into her again. She tightened around him. "I want to keep you there and soak in the lust oozing from you."

Holt's deep groan and *oooh* sent waves rolling between them. Holt's eyes caught hers. The spark in his ignited the bonfire she could no longer deny. Mutual lust mixed with caring, wanted expression. Words failed her. His tenderness melted any icy resolve remaining within her. Her heart cried out the words she didn't feel she could speak aloud. *I love you, Holt Addison.*

Chapter Ten

Torrey groaned, clenching Holt's arms as he glided deeper into her. The man knew how to bring a woman to the edge on the first thrust. He teased her G-spot until she gasped and pushed against him. "Yes," she hissed as the wave of her first orgasm claimed her.

Holt's breath swirled around her ear as his wordless response rushed out of him. She tightened up as another wave of pleasure rushed over her and dropped her in the midst of another huge orgasm.

Torrey felt and heard Holt's sharp intake. She arched her fingers and, began dragging her nails slowly down his back with his next breath. His shuddered exhale and fast jerk of his hips told her that her actions got what she wanted, a rise in his desire and a reaction that spurred him on. As Holt's head rose, she caught his earlobe with her lips and sucked.

"Ooh, that is n–nice," Holt stammered, pulling his head away. "Ah, darling, I'm real close."

Torrey reached for the pillow closest to her. She needed it under her head. If Holt got much harder, he'd pop for sure. She wanted to feel him reaching his pleasure. The condom wouldn't permit much feeling. Whatever was possible, she wanted and needed it. The more Holt touched her and reacted to her touch, the more Torrey knew she was in danger of losing her heart. For now, she refused to focus on that potentiality.

"Holt," she whispered, arching up against him as she settled back on the pillow. "I'm ready to come together."

Holt rose up. His hands tightly beside Torrey helped keep his weight from pressing her further into the mattress. Grinding his hips against hers, he winked.

"Love, are you sure?" Holt eased partway out of Torrey. "If I change up the angle to the one you love and stroke you like this." He reached between her legs and found her swollen clit. He rolled the plump pearl between his thumb and finger. Torrey's sharp gasp got him harder. If this was good now, when he got her boiling again without condoms...Holt swallowed hard. His heart skipped a beat every time she moaned and moved against him.

"Yes," Torrey groaned, reaching for the pillow beneath her head. She clutched part of it in her fisted hand.

Holt grinned, inhaled, and high-fived himself mentally. He remembered the first time he'd gotten her this hot and bothered. That led to their friends-with-benefits connection. This time he planned on a permanent connection. No fleeting dates or spurts of dates, planned or spontaneous, either. He wanted Torrey as his girlfriend, them known as a couple in a committed relationship, maybe more beyond that.

Holt dipped his head, brushed his lips over Torrey's, and nibbled his way along her jawline. Every breath she took brought her aroused nipples tighter against him. As they grazed over his, his breathing shook with two quick inhalations. It was like a shared bolt of heady need zapped through each of them and ricocheted backward with each breath he took.

As he reached her ear, Torrey arched her neck as another small orgasm hit her. God, he loved how she rolled from one peak of pleasure to another once her sensual side ignited. Her growing wetness told him she was close to a large orgasm. He wanted her there again.

"Grab another pillow," Holt murmured between suckles of Torrey's earlobe. He worried the small piece of flesh between his teeth. He let go and blew gently over the moist flesh. If she tightened much more around him, there was no holding back. "Easy with those wonderful muscles. I want this as much as you do."

Torrey's muffled "uh-huh" and shaky movements halted Holt's actions. Getting the other pillow under her hips would give him the angle and access he needed. He rose partway up, using one of his arms to gain the leverage he needed to see what Torrey was doing.

Torrey swore her insides turned liquid when Holt said, "Get another pillow." His memory of how, what, and where amazed her. It was as though he'd not forgotten a bit of what turned her on, how things enhanced her orgasms, and where his touches skyrocketed her desire to volcanic levels. She grabbed the first pillow her hand reached.

Her next breaths stammered through her as she felt more of the pillow. The plump, decorative neck roll pillow. That would raise her hips enough to give Holt the angle he loved best. He could pull partway out and tease her clit. The look on his face as she nudged the pillow against his hand said he had additional ideas. Torrey inhaled deeply and let go. Holding back was no longer an option.

Holt licked his lips as the pillow Torrey chose came into sight. He felt and knew her reaction before he even saw which one. Oh, yes this was the one for sure. She'd have the support she needed without the give that the firmer, larger ornate pillows wouldn't provide. Her squirming grew the more he licked and rubbed his lips together in anticipation. Even their silent communication hadn't lapsed. One more check on the growing list that told his heart she was the one.

"I got it, sweetie." Holt tugged the pillow to them. The only way he would get Torrey comfortably positioned was to pull out. He doubted she'd cool that much, given the heat cuddling him inside her. He rolled to his side, easing his exit while carefully holding the condom covering his cock in place and ensuring he continued touching her.

"When I stand up, roll to your side and pull your legs up. That way you can raise up enough for me to slip this under you." Holt patted the pillow. He scooted to the end of the mattress and turned as he rose.

Torrey's fair skin stood out against the dark-rose sheets. Her flushed face and neck added to his heat more than she knew. Even down to the tops of her breast, the flush continued. Score one for the team, his ego cried. Holt kept his thoughts to himself. Chastising his ego out loud wouldn't look good and might have Torrey thinking he changed his mind. As she moved, her hair tousled more. More spikes appeared. She appeared edgy and thoroughly turned on. Her scent pummeled him as she braced her feet on the mattress, lifting her hips.

"Here, let me help you." He leaned down, taking the pillow from her, and held it to her hips. "Slowly lower yourself as I bring the pillow down until you touch it again." Kneeling between Torrey's legs, he guided his cock back into place.

Torrey tried to lie still. Her clit pulsed every time Holt touched her, turning her on in ways she hadn't realized before. Maybe before she'd been in it for her rewards without thinking more about the other person involved. Thoughts flew in random directions as Holt stroked back into her.

"No one knows me like you do," she breathlessly commented. "It's like we've never been apart."

Holt's smile brought her internal volcano to eruption. He picked up the pace as she began thrusting toward him. Every stroke sent more lava flowing out followed by sparks. The tenderness in his eyes along with his airborne kiss enveloped her in their tight spiral of desire and need. Her eyes closed as the first wave of orgasm flooded her.

Holt rose up on one arm. Working his hand between them, he found Torrey's clit. It throbbed in rhythm to the pace they set. Lubricating his fingertips with her growing wetness, he fondled her. He used his knees to gain a steeper angle. On his next plunging in, he gently squeezed her clit and flicked it rapidly.

Torrey's hips rose off the pillow and met him thrust for thrust. It was as though he never pulled out of her. She met his retreat with her own forward motion. Her last gasp propelled him headfirst into his release. His balls tightened, and with one more stroke, Torrey arched to him, crying out as she clenched him deep inside her.

White light burst around him as his eyes slammed closed. Ripples of bright colors dotted the dark and rose up as he dove headlong into the hard orgasms washing over him.

Holt caught himself before he collapsed on Torrey. He quickly slid his arm around her waist and rolled her with him on their sides. The neck roll pillow shot into the air, bounced off the headboard and onto the floor. Torrey's giggles vibrated his neck. Holt snorted. This is what he missed with others he'd been with, the connection and intimate sharing after sex. *You mean lovemaking, dude*, his conscience nudged. Holt cracked one eye open. He rolled both heavenward and stuck his tongue out. He didn't care what fate called what they'd done. He knew it was more than fucking or a quickie. Verbalizing it would wait for a while longer, Holt decided. His eyes refused to stay open.

Torrey smiled as Holt's breathing slowed. She could hear his heart slow as well. The strong lub-a-dub soothed her. She knew an easiness with Holt that no other man ever brought her. She'd deal with her heart and conscience later. Her eyes fluttered closed as her breathing deepened.

Loud shrill barks and yowls filled the silence. The noise grew in volume, tossing Torrey awake. Shoving her hands into her hair, she blinked. Holt snored softly on his side. She yawned, wanting to ignore the fiasco happening in the hall. She didn't care which one of the motley trio had started things. She was going to finish it. Slipping from the bed carefully to not wake Holt, Torrey stood up. She reached the bedroom doorway as she finished belting her robe.

"Mischa, shhh. Doxie, quiet," Torrey began, opening the door wider. Siam's yowls grew in intensity as Torrey stepped out the door. Looking down the hall, she jumped back, flattening herself against the wall. Siam raced down the hall as if the hounds of hell were after him. Mischa and Doxie gave pursuit as fast as their short legs allowed. Their nails clicked across the tile floor, mixing with each bark.

Siam sped through the open door and leapt toward the dresser closest to him. Mischa skidded to a halt as she hit the carpet in past the doorjamb. Doxie flipped over her and rolled until she knocked the bed frame, yelping in pain.

Siam jumped off the path of dressers he crossed and down onto the bed. Mischa nuzzled Doxie before she resumed barking. Torrey trotted across the room, trying to grab Doxie as she reached for Mischa. The bedframe decided it wanted to change dance partners and banged her toes.

"Damn, that hurts," Torrey hissed, clapping her hand over her mouth as her outburst echoed off the walls.

Holt bolted upright, shoved his hands through his hair, and spat out, "What the fuck is going on?"

Mischa sat up, begging, her tongue hanging out as her tail wagged. Doxie squirmed and wiggled. Siam glared at all of them as he plopped down on the stitched pillows near the headboard.

Torrey hopped on one foot, opening her mouth to speak. No words came out as the doorbell chimed twice.

Chapter Eleven

Holt bolted from the bed, stepping over Mischa and Doxie as he reached Torrey. "What have the hellions been up to?"

Before Torrey could answer, the doorbell chimed again.

"*Shit*, who could that be?" Holt leaned down and grabbed his silk boxers off the floor. They lay next to where he'd shucked his jeans the previous evening. Still slightly damp and clammy, he grimaced as he pulled them on.

Torrey's snickers didn't help his mood. After their harrowing time getting to her place, the need to take care of her, and then the motely trio, more sleep would do more than soothe his angry side. More slumber and Torrey snuggled to him would put him into balance on dealing with whatever aftermath the storm left behind.

"I'll get the door. You corral the hoodlums and feed them. I'll deal with you when I get back." Holt grabbed Torrey's arm, spun her to him, and brushed his lips over hers.

Torrey gulped twice. She opened her mouth to call out to Holt as he exited the bedroom. Before she could think of a smartass comeback, he'd disappeared from view. Siam's hiss followed by Mischa's yip forced her attention back to the villains at hand.

"I don't know what's gotten into you three." Torrey shook her finger at the three pairs of eyes watching her. "I've never seen you with this much cabin fever before."

She stuffed her feet into a pair of mule slippers by the dresser Siam used to make his escape. Mischa gave pursuit, followed by Doxie. Torrey sighed as she glanced in the mirror. She ran a brush through her hair. At least she didn't look like she'd just crawled out of bed. Tossing the brush on the dresser, she gave the bed one last longing look. She swore her heart lay there, waiting for Holt to come back and claim it.

"One moment," Holt called out, making his way across the cold kitchen tile floor. Sunlight beamed through the window. Holt shaded his eyes the closer he got. He'd popped his contacts out right after he'd put Torrey to bed last night. At least his gym bag sat untouched on the table where he'd dropped it after he located his contact case inside. He could make out the larger pieces of furniture and objects near him. Distance remained one huge blur.

He stopped as he reached the table. He unzipped the side pocket closest to him on his gym bag. He pulled out the extra glasses case he carried. A couple of wipes on his boxers later, he resumed his clearer trail to the front door.

As he skirted the pile of dog and cat toys, he couldn't help but smile. Torrey pampered her pets to a point. The plump pet pillows sat side by side. Dog and cat fur littered both. The motley trio shared. Holt's smile grew as he caught part of Torrey's scolding words and tone.

Firm yet warm and full of love. She'd be a great mother. At another point those thoughts would have curdled his stomach. Not now. Yes, Torrey at his side raising their brood together. A vision flashed through him. Torrey, the dogs, and a twin stroller walked toward him. Holt swallowed hard, picking up his pace. He had his work cut out for him if that vision was to come true.

A hard knock sounded as Holt neared the door. He reached for the doorknob when Torrey called out.

"Holt, wait up. I'm pretty sure I know who that is."

Torrey touched Holt's elbow as she came up beside him. "That's either Mrs. Giddings, my elderly neighbor two doors down or..." Torrey's voice trailed off.

"Okay," Holt answered. "Who else are you expecting?"

If her hunky male model neighbor Miguel was out there...Christ, she didn't need two male egos gearing up for battle. Miguel's partner Steve teased her and Miguel about their hot attraction. Friends, nothing more. Miguel saw her as the little sister he never had. Lord, the man could be overly protective.

"Well, who else?" Holt groaned as another knock sounded simultaneously with two long blasts on the door chime.

"Best let me answer." Torrey shoved her way in front of Holt.

"Wait and be..." Holt started.

Torrey flipped the lock, opening the door, ignoring the rest of Holt's words.

"Are you Ms. Neadson?" The gray-haired man standing on her porch seemed familiar. She couldn't put a name with his face.

"Depends on who wants to know." Holt's voice boomed over her shoulder.

Torrey bit the inside of her bottom lip, stifling her comeback. Sure, she could look after herself. Her known neighbors called her by name, not a formal address.

Torrey knew Holt wanted to protect her. Take care of her was the term that came to mind. Echoes of past heated discussions popped up here and there as the man on the porch gave Holt the once-over. Holt's muscles tightened under her hand as she reached back and touched him. Great, now she had another male deciding she needed safeguarding. She squeezed his arm hard and let go. Enough already. She was okay, and until the dude made a move, she didn't need that kind of assistance.

"How can I help?" Torrey waved, hoping to catch the man's attention.

He nodded and spoke. "I moved in a few days ago. I'm renting from my son for the next few months. He mentioned you lived here and might help me with getting settled in. Your community connections were the one thing he emphasized."

Torrey smiled and stepped forward. She held out her hand. "You're Jon's dad. Welcome to Cascade Bay."

"Thanks. I would have waited to introduce myself. Last night's storm blew out the power for many folks and stranded some. I've checked on people up and down the street. There's no way out until the water goes down under the bridge or the flooding recedes." He shook her hand briefly. He turned to Holt, who had worked his way between the door and Torrey.

Torrey inhaled, quickly counted to five, and exhaled. "I appreciate the information. Are you okay?"

Holt's hand cupped her ass through her robe. His thumb rubbed up and down the crack separating the cheeks. She pushed his hand away. He brought it right back, almost swatting her firmly as he did. She bit the inside of her bottom lip again. The man was working up to a tirade. One she was going to love giving.

The gent smiled. "I'm fine. If you folks need anything, come on over. I've got two of the elderly neighbors bunking with me for now. Glad to know you're all right. Good-bye."

Holt stopped fondling Torrey's ass. The old gent appeared harmless. Holt took two quick breaths. He'd felt Torrey stiffen the moment he touched her. Every moment mattered to him. They'd become precious since they'd made love. Yes, a few intimate moments confirmed what his stubborn heart refused to hear. No matter what his conscience dredged up, past experiences were that, done and over with. He wanted another chance with them as a couple. Would she being willing to hear him out? Or give them another try?

He sighed as Torrey walked away from him. Her stiff posture said something irked her. He hoped her temper cooled by the time she faced him. Her prior tirades had scorched and singed more than he liked. Back then, neither of them refrained from speaking out. Bad feelings and harsh words had weakened what they had at the height of their friendship. Better to go after her and get things hashed out. They were stuck for the next few days whether they liked it or not.

"Torrey, wait up please," Holt called out, following behind her. "We need to talk."

By the time he reached the hall, he heard the bathroom door slam shut. Slumped against the wall, memories of a similar argument leapt up. Holt clenched his fists. Damn, he'd done it again. Probably would a few more times until they came to an understanding. Possibly, with mutual respect, time and experience would work for them instead of against either of them. Why did he feel such an overwhelming need to protect her?

"Torrey," Holt called through the closed door. "I'm sorry."

A muffled yell and cursed reply sounded behind the door. Thuds and whacks followed before a grim-faced Torrey opened the door.

"You're *sorry*?" Torrey's flushed cheeks cut Holt deep into his heart. He'd seen her mad. This was angry and not in a good way. The iciness of her tone and emphasis on "sorry" raised goose bumps on his bare skin. Holt backed away from the door as Torrey stepped toward him.

Torrey heaved an exasperated huff. Holt's apology caught her off guard. She didn't want him to back off what he felt. They needed to discuss what happened. Yes, her ire wanted to fight and yell. She'd grown beyond this in the last two years. A calm discussion probably wouldn't ensue, but a get-it-out-in-the-open one needed to happen.

She inhaled and exhaled slowly, forcing her thoughts to focus on the here and now. Not the past. Her rational side wanted her to calm down even more. While her angered part kept poking its tines into her, she knew staying upset wouldn't facilitate what needed saying. She reached toward Holt. Two yips and a sharp yowl echoed down the hall.

She couldn't help smiling if she wanted to. The trio sounded like her except two of them had pent-up energy and the third was tired of the other two plucking his nerve. Holt's wary look didn't help to stifle the giggles threatening to burst out.

"Holt," Torrey began, waving him toward her. "The charge is about to resume. Get out of the way, okay?"

Holt moved toward her, shrugging as a he opened his mouth. "Charge?"

He no more than got the words out as she grabbed his arm and pulled him to her. A quick glance toward the bedroom said they were safe for the moment. A whitish-brown blur raced by, followed by two medium-brown ones in hot pursuit.

Holt grunted as he landed against her. Torrey drew her eyes back to his. His arms bulged as he braced himself against the doorjamb, keeping his full weight off her. "What is with them?" He shook his head, winking as he dipped his head toward her.

"Pent-up angst and—" Holt's lips brushed over hers, preventing further speech. His warm breath rushed over her face as she tipped her head back, allowing him greater access to her mouth. Two quick puckers occurred before he pulled away as her tongue pressed against his lips.

Holt broke off the kiss as the tip of Torrey's tongue brushed his lips. As much as he wanted her again, taking advantage of the moment didn't feel right. The old Holt would have grabbed it with gusto and not thought twice about things. Maybe afterward he might have. Studying for the bar exam and his internship at Gwen's shelter along with the public defender cases he'd taken until he decided to set up his own practice taught him life dealt hands that weren't always easy or nice. More often, it was grimy and messy like the poor woman they saw last night.

He rested his forehead on Torrey's. "Love, I think the trio needs taking care of before anything else." He smiled as his stomach grumbled. "Then food and coffee for us. Sound good?"

Torrey's brief nod and small grin reduced some of the anguish he felt. He knew nothing changed until they talked and perhaps fought. More like a heated discourse, as Stuart's Grandma Getty used to put it when Stuart's folks dropped him off for a few days. Holt turned and walked toward the kitchen, hesitating only briefly until he heard Torrey's footsteps behind him. Two years ago, they were different people in age and maturity. Could they bridge that gap and find an *us* that made as much sense as making love earlier had?

Chapter Twelve

Torrey halted by the double sliding glass doors leading to her patio and fenced backyard. "Mischa, here. Doxie, come."

Siam ran by her, leapt on the counter closest to him, and up on top of the refrigerator. He quickly tucked his tail under him and leered down at all he surveyed. Torrey shook her head, smiled, and glanced down to her feet. Mischa and Doxie wiggled every time their tails wagged. "Outside, you two."

Torrey pulled open the blinds covering the doors. She shaded her eyes as she unlocked the sliders. "Oh, my. Holt, you better come see this."

Mischa and Doxie raced past her as she slid one door partway open. Both made their way to the closest mud puddle they could find. Torrey sighed as Holt reached her side.

"Looks like we'll be bathing two dogs after breakfast." Holt's soft chuckle drew Torrey's attention. She continued, "I did say we, didn't I?"

"What about the feline vulture?" Holt pointed at Siam glaring at them from his lofty perch. His tail twitched back and forth as though he plotted something.

"Do you see him making a beeline for the door or the mud?" Torrey winked at Holt. "The cat has some sense. I wonder why he torments those two like he does. I suspect they torment him, too."

Holt chortled at Torrey's conspirator wink. "If reading feline or canine minds were that simple and easy."

He eased his arm around her waist and pulled her to him. She cuddled to him as if she'd accepted his apology. He knew better than to believe that. Torrey forgave easily when she didn't feel cornered. Not that he had done that earlier. Keeping his hand on her in an intimate way established his presence. Probably a bit more dominantly than either of them needed or wanted. Holt moved away from Torrey. He wanted—no, make that needed coffee and food before he tackled their earlier trouble.

"While we can, how about we get breakfast?" Holt moved toward the coffeemaker he'd spotted on his way through the kitchen. "It's been hours since we ate."

Torrey's shrug immobilized him. Her indifference didn't feel right. Nothing he could put his finger firmly on came to mind. Her cussing and frowning as she came out the bathroom yelled her frustration and anger louder than if she'd said the words to him. Why was she acting aloof? Holt turned, walked two more steps...Shit, she was hiding behind her calm façade. He was in deep trouble if he didn't get her talking soon. Torrey's slow burn could rise to volcanic proportions if left uncontrolled. He knew better than to let on what he'd figured out. The sooner he got them eating and more coherent, the better off both of them were.

"I'll get the coffee started," Holt offered. He remembered how Torrey took her coffee. Hot, sweet, and two dashes of cream. Not half-and-half. She took real cream in her coffee. The smile on her face the day they located the organic local dairy near their university campus stayed with him. He loved the unabashed joy in her eyes as she sipped the coffee the owner's wife served them with the homemade sweets they'd purchased. Torrey's sweet tooth rivaled his. He hoped she had plenty of goodies in supply.

Torrey snickered at Holt's offer. "You still can't cook, can you?" She teased him every time he'd asked her over before. His usual offer of ordering in or warming up something in the microwave kept his bachelor habits secret until she said no one evening.

"I might have learned." Holt flashed a grin before he began filling the coffeemaker with water. "You make the best pancakes I've had. Even Grandma Getty wanted your recipe. Which you never did share."

"Like I was going to give up the one thing I knew you kept coming back for besides sex?" Torrey opened the refrigerator and looked inside. "Seeing as I'm cooking, simple and easy is our best option."

Holt faced her, clutching his stomach and groaning. "You mean my poor tummy must languish more without those delicious morsels?"

Torrey giggled, shaking her head. "For now. I'm famished. Burned a few calories this morning. Besides, Mischa and Doxie aren't going to stay out there very long. They don't like being cold and wet."

She set the coffee and things needed to prep their meal on the counter next to Holt. As she went about finding the rest of the items she needed to finish cooking their eggs, bacon, and toast, a familiar feeling settled over her. She glanced over her shoulder at Holt standing at the sink, drying the few dishes he'd washed from her prior meals. The man didn't hesitate to pitch in. The warm contentment filling her felt right. A sense of déjà vu enveloped her. Torrey blinked twice, glanced at Holt again, and inhaled sharply. They'd been this close right before he started seeing another woman.

Crap, *merde*, and shit in every other foreign language she'd learned to say it in. It was happening again...or was it? Torrey worried her bottom lip between her teeth. Two years ago, she almost gave him her heart. Time and experience changed people. Had he? The tenderness and passion of his physical intimacy hadn't been as apparent then. This morning he'd made love, not fucked. Not that Holt had ever been entirely a fucker and not a lover. What surprises awaited her this time? What secrets he hadn't shared?

Yes, what secrets? Great, even her psyche joined the protesters chanting vigorously in her heart and head. Her gut sided with her cautious side. Every time she stepped back from her growing feelings, her stomach subsided and bits of sanity seemed to return. *Do you fear the unknown?*

Torrey glanced over her shoulder. Only Holt stood behind her pulling coffee mugs from the cabinet where she kept them. She believed in guardian angels and being watched over. Which one of the angels was trying to get a message through?

Holt clicked on the radio sitting on the counter near the coffeemaker. Torrey fumbled with the carton of eggs in her hands and gasped as music filled the kitchen. Lyrics from the Bee Gees's song "I've Gotta Get a Message to You" danced around her, enveloping her within every nuance and measure. As the chorus of the song began, Torrey sniffled. She didn't know whether tears of uncertainty threatened or tears of suppressed laughter. Either one she couldn't explain because she didn't have the words or complete thoughts to begin with. Taking short breaths, she placed the eggs on the stove next to the skillet cooking the bacon.

"Holt," she said, turning to where he stood. "Can you get me the bowl in the cabinet where the cups are?" His quiet nod and ease of movements rushed over her in a wave of calm. His warm look and natural actions felt right, like he'd done this before. Truth was, he had but with different intentions and...Oh hell, she needed coffee and food before she tried to figure out what everything meant. If her guardian angels wanted her at ease with him, so be it. For now, she needed to focus on cooking and not dissecting the chemistry pulsing between them.

As she mixed the eggs and cream, she snuck one last look at Holt leaning against the counter, sipping his coffee as though he'd done it a million times before. He raised his cup and saluted her. Torrey swallowed hard and quickly turned back to her cooking. She willed herself to visualize icicles dangling off her patio overhang. A cool interior would help her deal with the boiling exterior heat waiting to capture her again.

Holt pushed back from the table forty minutes later. "You make a good mini omelet. You remembered how I liked my bacon done. Folding it into the eggs gave them the extra taste they needed. My compliments to the cook." He raised his empty coffee mug. "Another pot?"

Torrey's eyes didn't meet his. Her muffled "sure" didn't sound convincing. He wanted to hug her and whisper that all was okay. Maybe everything was wonderful? Shit, how did he go about reassuring her when he couldn't say where they went from here? They needed to clear the air over the past and decide where they wanted to go next. Holt rose and moved toward the sink with his dishes. As he reached the counter, two high-pitched yips and howls sounded. So much for the opening remarks he'd thought of.

"How muddy are they?" He set his dishes in the sink, catching Torrey's frown out of the corner of his eye. "Do we catch them as they come in or what?"

Torrey's short laugh and shake of her head said he'd missed the needed action. "They will bound in no matter what we do. They can remain out there a few minutes more. We need better traction than my slippers and your bare feet."

She rose, motioning for him to follow. "Grab your sneakers and come with me."

Holt unzipped his gym bag, found his sneakers, and trotted down the hall after Torrey. Outside the bathroom, he dropped one shoe, hopped on one foot trying to get the other on. "What about you?"

Torrey turned from where she rummaged in the towel-lined shelves. "I've got deck shoes in my closet. Best to have the towels and soap ready. They hate baths as much as they love mud."

Holt snickered at Torrey's last line. "Sounds like kids for sure. I'll grab your shoes. You get the tub running. We'll corral the hoodlums as they dash in. Can we herd them into here?"

"Say the word treats, show them a dog biscuit or two, and they will follow you. Keeping them in here is another thing. I'll wait behind the door to close it once they're in."

"Great, I get the dirty job." He grinned as Torrey tossed a towel at him.

"You get part of it. We'll be lucky if we don't need two baths when we're done with them. Hope you got a change of clothes in that bag."

Holt shrugged. "I'll worry about that once those two are washed and dried."

"Get my deck shoes before you go back out in the kitchen. I will get the tub running. Oh, make sure Siam is out of the way, too. Last time I had mud all over my living room furniture, carpet, and tables. Chase the cat is a favorite game when they come in from outside."

Holt laughed as he trotted down the hall after tying his shoes snugly. "I'll do my best to keep that from happening."

Torrey's smile and wink told him she enjoyed his humor. "Thanks for getting my shoes." She tossed her slippers on the shelf closest to her. "The dog biscuits are in the pantry near the door. The long door cabinet is the one."

"Got it," Holt called out, making his way into the kitchen. "Be back in a moment."

Several waves of the treats he held and a few calls got Mischa and Doxie where they wanted them, cornered in the bathroom. Ten towels, lots of soap, and a few "oopses" later, two clean dogs raced out the door toward the living room.

Chapter Thirteen

Holt looked down the front of him. Muddy streaks and clumps of dirt clung to him. His silk boxers resembled a kindergartener's finger painting adventure. His shoes looked like he'd hiked five miles through water and dirt. He glanced at the mirror in front of him. His hair stood up on end worse than if he'd styled it that way. Streaks of dirt crisscrossed his face in a pattern he didn't remember making as he wiped his sweaty face on his arm numerous times.

Torrey couldn't contain her mirth. "Lord, Holt you look like you had a mud fight with those two."

His snort and chortle drew her attention. He pointed at her reflection in the mirror. "I'd say you got the worse of the wear, if you ask me."

Torrey shook her head. Two huge brown spots marred her white terrycloth bathrobe. Dirty streaks ran up and down the arms and onto her hands. "That is why I do with wash and wear more than anything else. Easy to clean and no worries."

"Suits don't take well to washers." Holt grinned as he gathered up the wet soggy towels. "Where do you want these?"

Torrey led him into the smaller bedroom off the hall. Opening the double doors near her, she pointed to the washer. "In there, please."

As she untied her robe, she caught Holt's inquisitive look. "What's got your interest?"

"I'm wondering what I'm supposed to do about these." He pointed to his boxers. "I have my gym shorts and T-shirt I can wear. Without underwear, I'm not going there. Commando ain't my style."

Torrey bit her lip to keep from blurting out her answer. She knew Holt hated feeling conspicuous. If he wore the same type of workout shorts as he used to, when he bent over, nothing would be left to her imagination. "You wearing the same workout shorts?"

Holt's infectious grin, the shaking of his head, and his quick shrug told her nothing. Torrey sighed and rolled her eyes. "Okay, I get my faux pas. You couldn't be wearing the same shorts unless you got enough pairs to last you a few years."

"Actually, I found out that if I wanted children, I needed to wear less constraining ones." Holt dumped his armload of towels in the washer. "Truth is I also prefer to not chafe areas that can get sensitive."

Torrey dropped her robe on top of the towels, added detergent, and started the load. "I believe I got an answer to your problem."

She led the way back out into the hall, stopping in front of another small closest near her bedroom. "Joanna and I run a foundation on the side as part of our business. We wanted to give back to the community as well as to ensure the community knew we were more than another adult-oriented business. Since Gwen needed funding and we could help, we got together."

Holt nodded. He reached for one of the double-door handles. "Gwen told me about your generosity around the holidays and other times. How can this help me?"

"Let me show you." Torrey pushed Holt's hand aside. "We collect gently used clothing and other personal items. We get in men's items as well as women's." She reached in and pulled out a stack of male briefs with the price tags still on them. "See if you can find a pair or two in there. In my closet is a bag of laundered clothes that aren't sorted yet. You might find something in there, too."

Torrey started toward her bedroom. "I'm tired of looking like Mischa and Doxie used me as their mud puddle diving board. Let me grab some clothes, shower, and dress. You can use the guest bath, if you want."

Holt waited until he heard the click of the bathroom door before he moved to Torrey's closet. In the past two years, she'd grown a lot. Previously, she gave to charities and staunchly said let them do the work. Now she ran her own and made sure she gave back to the community that supported her with business and a home. One thing stood out in his mind. Why was she single? No one appeared in contention with him. Even Gwen's recent comment about Torrey attending charity fundraisers alone seemed odd to him. Torrey never lacked for attention or dates before they began hooking up or even after they settled into friends.

He tossed two pairs of underwear in his size on the bed. Tidy whites would do. He made a mental note to replace them and get ongoing supplies delivered for the shelter she provided for.

As he opened the closet, he noticed the variety and hues of color hanging before him. Torrey had grown in another way. Her previous clothing array lacked any of the vibrancy and pattern these did. Her monochromatic tops hung near print blouses and skirts. He noticed the blazers toward the rear of the closet. A deep gold shade drew his eyes toward an item hanging near it. The print looked familiar.

The textured design reminded him of a shirt he had a few years back. Where had she found this? Faded and worn aside, he remembered his love of the color and how many compliments he'd gotten every time he wore the shirt. Curious, he pulled the hanger from the rack. As he brought it closer, a ragged white tag inside the collar caught his attention.

"I'll be—" Holt whistled. "You kept it. I thought I lost this. Now I know where I left it. This tells me a whole lot more."

Holt thrust the hanger back on the rack as he heard the shower cut off. He stepped back, looking for the bag Torrey mentioned. He saw it under the shirt he'd put back. Talk about coincidence. He dumped the contents on the bed. Shirts of various sizes fell out, followed by jeans. Holt folded the items as he laid them aside. Two changes of clothes remained. The faded slogan T-shirts and jeans would do until his were clean. He smiled as he held the jeans up. He hadn't worn high waters since junior high school.

"Good, you found some things."

Holt turned and faced a towel-wrapped Torrey.

"Oh yeah, I sure did. Brought back a few memories, too." Holt tossed the jeans on the bed next to the shirts. "Leave me any warm water? I doubt there's any hot."

Torrey smiled, rolled her eyes, and snapped Holt with her towel. "Plenty of *hot* water. I replaced the tank with a larger one when I remodeled the patio and kitchen last year."

Toweling her hair more, she moved toward Holt. No matter how much her gut and heart tugged her back and forth, she needed his touch and warmth. They survived nature's wrath and a furious storm. Dodged lightning and trees as part of their survival. She didn't care about logic or her usual rants about wanting more. She wanted—no, desired—his presence. To feel him wrapped around her, holding her tight against him and reassuring her things would be all right.

Torrey inhaled and let go a deep sigh. She dropped the towel as she stood toe-to-toe with Holt. Tilting her head back, she closed her eyes and puckered. She didn't care how silly she might look or how contradictory it was to any of her earlier thoughts or actions. Right now, her world ran off-kilter. Only Holt's kiss and hug could correct that.

Moments passed. Nothing happened. She counted, fighting the urge to open her eyes. Could she face him if he stood there looking at her? Or moved away? Torrey inhaled and...

Holt crushed her to him. His lips scalded hers as he possessively deepened the kiss. His hands slid in opposite directions of each other. One firmly cupped her ass. The other cradled her head.

Torrey pressed tighter against Holt. Her arms slipped around his waist. She opened her lips, wanting to taste him again. Mud and dirt didn't matter. He did, and the comfort he gave consoled her in ways she didn't realize she missed.

His tongue brushed against hers. She drank deeply, rolling his masculine taste over her taste buds and enjoying each nuance that came through. His coffee laced with sugar and a touch of cream led, followed by a hint of pepper and hot sauce. How he loved tasty spices mixed with his food. Lastly, the sweet blackberry jam she made flowed in, adding its distinct accent. Torrey inhaled, drawing Holt's scent deep into her lungs. Male sweat mixed with sexual desire flooded her.

Torrey swallowed hard as Holt's lips closed over hers. Strong need threatened to overwhelm her. What was it with her? Only a few hours had passed since they'd made love. Her orgasms left her weak kneed and unable to think coherently for quite a few moments. How could she be ready to take Holt back to bed? Was she ready to start all over again?

She didn't want to halt the feeling of security enveloping her. Her thoughts refused to let go of the physical want pulsing through her. Trying to get her eyes to open, Torrey attempted to pull back. Holt's fingers tangled in her hair, holding her in place. He didn't want to stop or slow down. She had no choice. She had to take control.

Torrey turned her head sideways. "Stop. Please, Holt. Stop."

Holt broke off the kiss, pulling his lips away from Torrey's. His short breaths punctuated his emotions. Resting his forehead on hers, he inhaled deeply and opened his eyes. He blinked, trying to get Torrey back in focus. His glasses fogged more with each breath. "God, I love having you in my arms like this. But I can't see you, and your tone says you need me to see you."

"Please," Torrey sighed. "Sorry to get things heated up without results."

Holt released Torrey and stepped away. "Don't be. It's not like I've got a case of blue balls happening. I've learned restraint and control."

Torrey's weak laugh lessened the distress he felt. Another feeling rushed into his mind. Joy grew as the thought took form. They'd talked and gotten through a rough patch without a full-blown argument. They still needed to talk and work things out.

"Look, you got messed up again. Let me go shower in the other bathroom while you sponge off and get dressed. I'm hankering for another cup of coffee and some more of that jam." Torrey bent and picked up her towel.

Holt fisted his hand closest to her. He itched to reach out and touch her. To slide his fingers down the curve of her ass and slip inside her cleft, teasing her clit until she squirmed with pleasure. He slowly lowered his hand, clenching his fist tighter as he fought the urge to fondle her. Their lovemaking was hot and sweet this morning. He wanted to keep things that way. Until they discussed their earlier angst, sex took a backseat. He hoped it didn't try to drive from there.

He grabbed one of the shirts and a pair of jeans off the bed. "Toss me a pair of briefs, please. I'm tired of dirt and mud. See you in the kitchen in a few."

Holt caught the briefs Torrey tossed in midair. "Thanks." He turned and trotted out of the room. The sooner he got a cool shower running, the better his libido would behave.

Torrey watched and admired the way Holt's buns moved when he ran. Seeing his exaggerated movements as he left the room got her heated in more ways than she cared to admit. Fanning herself, she walked to her dresser. She added underwear and shorts to the top she pulled from off the hanger. Careful not to brush against the clothes draped over her arm, she made her way back into the bathroom. Holt's off-key singing screeched out from the guest bath. She laughed as he tried to reach the high note of a favorite song from the eighties. The man could croon with the best of them when he chose to. His antics teased her even without him directly saying so. He knew she referred to his falsetto as nails raking across a blackboard. As long as Mischa and Doxie didn't start howling or barking, Torrey wouldn't comment.

Chapter Fourteen

As Torrey entered the kitchen fifteen minutes later, she caught bits and pieces of the tune Holt sang as he apparently dried off. He sang a love song, one that he'd written while they dated. The one he'd dedicated to her. Torrey swallowed hard and reached for the coffeemaker.

Her hand trembled as she gripped the pot. Holt said when he wrote the song, he knew the girl in it was the one for him. He dedicated the song to her using her name as filler. Joanna kept telling her over the years that Holt really meant the song for her and wrote it about her.

Torrey filled the pot, put two scoops of coffee in the filter, and poured the water into the top of the maker. As much as she wanted to comment on Holt's singing, she knew better. If she said something about the song, he'd bring up why he sang it. The loudness of his voice indicated she heard him no matter what. Not mentioning it seemed like her best option.

"Holt, coffee's on. I'm setting out more homemade bread and jam," Torrey called over her shoulder. Wonderful aromas filled the air as the bread warmed in the microwave. Cinnamon mixed with wheat berry tantalized her taste buds. She added butter to the items sitting on the table. Holt's footsteps sounded as he entered the kitchen.

Torrey turned around and began giggling. "Lord, Holt," she spat out in between outburst of laughter. "I didn't realize how short those were."

Holt glanced down. The hem of the jean legs barely reached the lower third of his calf. His bare feet added to the picture of humor he imagined Torrey saw. "Well, don't say I didn't warn you. It's not bad. At least they aren't tight. Whoever donated these must have lost weight or been very short." Holt pulled the waistband out, showing how much room he had.

"How are you keeping them up?" Torrey's arched eyebrows and open mouth set him off laughing. As Holt gasped for air, he pointed to his belt in his other hand.

"Here let me help you with that before you lose them all together!" Torrey set the cup she held on the counter and quickly closed the space between them. Holt tried to stop laughing. The worried look on her face set him to snickering as she reached him. He inhaled sharply as her frown appeared.

Torrey pulled the belt from his hand. She shook her finger at him as she spoke. "Look here, Holt Addison."

"Yes, ma'am." He worried the inside of his lower lip with his teeth. He loved when Torrey lost her cool because that spark led to some steamy sex as they made up. Today was different. He needed her calm and composed. Their discussion couldn't be put off.

Torrey threaded his belt through the loops and cinched it extra snug. She stuck her tongue out at him. He couldn't resist. Holt swung Torrey up in his arms and nibbled her tongue. He pressed his lips full on hers, seeking entrance to her mouth. Torrey squirmed against him. Even though she pushed and struggled to get away, she responded to him as her legs wrapped around him. Her hands tangled in his wet hair as she fisted clumps in them. Her mouth opened. Her tongue dueled with his. He followed her into her sweetness. Hints of minty toothpaste and mouthwash greeted him. The rough edges of her teeth grazed over the tops of his taste buds. Then she bit him.

"Ouch!" Holt jerked back. "What the—"

Torrey grinned and pounded her feet on his ass. "Put me down. I learned about self-defense while you were gone." She rocked back on her heels as Holt set her gently upright. "I'm sorry that happened. But sex isn't always going to solve things. I've learned that, too."

Holt nodded. "I'm sorry. Male hormones are all I can plead."

"Understood. Mine are moaning and wanting to whore again, too." Torrey walked back down the hall. "One minute."

She came back with two pairs of slipper socks. "Here. These will keep your feet warm." She tossed the blue pair at Holt.

She sat in the chair near her, pulled the red pair on, and pointed to the mugs. "I've got coffee made. Let's get the air cleared between us."

Holt's shrug worried Torrey. He usually spoke his mind, defended his stance, and kept his stubborn ego in the fight. Had she caught him that off guard? *Wow* didn't begin to describe the intense emotion filling her. Pride in her ability to surprise Holt mixed with pieces of fear and puffs of angst. What if she'd turned him off? Upset the balance between them? As she inhaled, Torrey reminded herself being alone wasn't awful. She had done well over the last two years, building her business and the foundation along with earning her master's degree in business administration. Still Holt's earlier line that suits didn't take well to washers either had her wondering.

"I promise not to bite." She offered Holt a wide grin, showing her teeth. "At least not where it would show. I've had my shots."

Holt couldn't resist Torrey's cheesy grin. She'd always had the power to break his bleakest moods with some corny line and funny face. He sank into the chair opposite her.

Steam rose from the mugs filled with coffee sitting middle of the table. Next to them lay two knives and spoons, a jar of jam, the butter dish, and containers of cream and sugar. Holt creamed and sugared his coffee as he watched Torrey pick up a slice of bread. "That smells good enough to eat without jam or butter. I didn't know you canned."

"I started six months ago. Joanna's brother lives on a couple of acres outside of town. He found blackberries and raspberries growing wild near the edge of his property. Instead of wasting the fruit we picked and preserved them," Torrey replied. Her nod and wink indicated her ire cooled enough to allow him to continue.

"I appreciate you putting up with me and my mistakes." Holt sipped his coffee. Warm sweetness filled his mouth and worked its way down his throat as he swallowed. He knew professionally to guard against pushing someone to talk before they were ready. Keeping his lawyer side under control wouldn't be easy unless he consciously focused on the here and now. Could he create a partnered discourse that invited her to express her feelings and openly say what she felt needed airing?

Torrey took a bite and chewed. She seemed to watch him as if she waited for him to say more. Lord, was this to be another one of their cat-and-mouse discussions? Waiting for the other to speak with moments of what felt like unceasing anxiety and silence?

Holt took another sip of coffee. He'd wait a bit longer. The smells of cinnamon and the fresh bread teased his nose and set his stomach to growling.

Torrey looked up. Holt's gaze moved over her as though he watched and needed something. She picked up the slices of fresh bread she'd put out. Holding the plate out to him, she nodded. He took the dish and set it before him. She needed a few more minutes to decide where she opened her questions. What mattered most to her? Why he wanted to make love or where he'd been in the last two years? Or was what mattered most why he felt the need to protect her when she'd answered the door? Several other questions rose with varying degrees of interest and pitfalls. Some concerning her reactions bothered her, too. One in particular made her cringe each time it echoed back amongst the others. How much did she really want to know?

Torrey picked up her mug and sipped. She grimaced as bitter black coffee swirled over her taste buds. She quickly sat the mug down. Reaching for the spoon near her, she looked up, catching Holt's smirk. She arched her eyebrow and gave him her best deadpan stare as she spooned sugar and cream into her coffee. As she stirred, she realized what she needed to know first.

"Why?" She set her spoon aside and reached for more bread. Holt's startled look made her want to lick five of her fingers and drag them downward through the air like she was marking a scoreboard. Score one for her anyway. She'd caught him off guard. A rarity for sure.

"Why what?" Holt's dull tone got her to add two points in his favor. Good thing he didn't know she started keeping an obscure tally.

"Why here and now? Why me after two years?" Torrey wiped off her spoon and laid it next to her.

Holt's deep breaths filled his chest as he chewed two bites of bread slathered with jam and butter. He wiped his mouth, drank coffee, and leaned back in his chair. Damn him! He wanted to play cat and mouse with her. Torrey started to fold her arms tight across her chest when he spoke.

"Here and now is rather obvious given the storm and its aftermath. Why you after two years?"

She nodded, motioning for Holt to continue.

"Happenstance. I knew you moved back from things Gwen told me. I figured you had someone. I didn't want to push things or upset what you had if you did."

Torrey inhaled sharply. Holt's last statement plunged deep into her. He cared enough to stay away. Her well-being mattered to him. She licked her lips and asked her next question. "Why did you show up last night?"

Holt's snicker irked her more than she wanted to let on. But, she couldn't keep the glare off her face.

Holt wanted to tease Torrey the more she glared at him. He knew he reached her when she didn't finish crossing her arms tightly in front of her. Her safety move he knew all too well. She tried to safeguard herself with that move as if her shields slammed into place, keeping things at bay. Her first question hadn't been one he'd counted on. He still didn't know why he'd agreed to accompany Stuart last night except another night at home watching reruns on TV or reading law journals made no sense. Getting out and being amongst people called to him in a way he couldn't quite explain. Maybe something outside of him urged him to put his caseload aside and refresh with others rather than choosing to hole up alone.

Holt remembered one of their fervent promises to each other. The one assurance that cemented their friendship from the start. No lying to each other. As times had proven, that was a hard promise to keep. The more they spoke their honesty, the more they trusted each other. Hell...Holt almost cussed aloud. He missed his other best friend, Torrey. How did he expose that?

Holt cleared his throat; looked up, and made sure he had Torrey's attention. "Remember our long-standing promise to be honest with each other no matter what?"

Torrey's brief nod and continued stare pricked him. He'd take a shot at putting his feelings on the table. "I had no idea what Stuart and Joanna had in mind. Stuart kept nagging me to get out. Said I needed to see what life outside work was like again."

Torrey toyed with her spoon before drinking more of her coffee. She leaned on her elbows, looking away as if she weighed what he said. Holt decided to continue. "After Stuart told me what they planned, I gave him an earful. Guilted him some with how he moaned and bitched about folks attempting to set him up with Joanna before they decided to get together on their own."

Torrey's grin said Holt struck pay dirt with her. He wet his lips and opened his mouth to speak. She held up her hand. "Let me guess," she offered.

Holt shrugged. "Sure. Go ahead."

"By then, you saw us and figured saying hello wouldn't hurt."

Holt burst out laughing. "Actually, it wasn't until I got a good look at the blonde server with the low-cut top next to you that I made my decision."

Torrey wadded up her napkin and threw it at him. "And here I thought you changed." She slumped down in her chair. A dejected look came over her face.

Holt sat upright and leaned forward. "The decision I made was you over anyone or anything else there, darlin'."

Holt's husky tone swirled around Torrey, seized her, and enveloped her before she realized it. Holt's answer stunned her and warmed her at the same time. She hadn't expected this nor could she have. As Holt stood, she emptied her mug. Her remaining questions shattered in comparison to his revelation.

Chapter Fifteen

"Let's sit in the living room." Holt offered Torrey his hand. He knew his last response didn't follow her line of thinking. Logic often didn't when one tried to surmise what the other was going to say or predict their actions. While he kept his lawyer side cooling its heels, he let his inquisitive part out.

Torrey took his hand and rose. "Let me clear the table first."

Holt tugged her to him. "Leave it for now. Nothing that can't wait beyond the cream and butter. I'll put them in the fridge. Go on and make yourself comfortable."

He put the cream and butter in the fridge He could feel Torrey intently watching him. Good. He had her attention. While he wanted to know why she bristled at him looking at the server, he knew pursuing that line directly wouldn't get them far. His male libido had looked. He had enjoyed the view and continued looking until he saw what he wanted, Torrey. Getting her to understand that was going to take some work. He sighed as he turned. She wasn't behind him. He spun toward the living room. She wasn't there either. Crap, where had she run off to? Hiding wasn't going to work. Holt turned as a loud clatter boomed down the hall.

"Shit," Torrey called out. "Now I have to spin them out again."

Holt started down the hall. "How can I help?"

"Put the cups in the sink, please. I forgot about to add the extra spin cycle to the load of towels and my robe. I'll be there in a moment."

As much as he wanted to check on her and help, Holt resisted the urge. He had to start trusting her as well as letting her ask for assistance when she needed it. Holt counted as he put away their snack and loaded the dishwasher. One of Torrey's favorite sayings repeated itself each time he heard her cuss. *Actions speak louder than words.* He needed to make his actions count.

Torrey sat on the bed in the guest room, waiting for the washer to start spinning again. She had missed the loud thump of the load going out of balance. Shaking her head, she leaned back on her hands. Her shorts edged higher, showing more of her thigh than she usually did. She started to reach toward the hem with one hand. Why? When had she turned so bloody conservative?

As the spin cycle picked up speed, she mulled over Holt's responses. He chose her over the server. That action floored her in ways she hadn't counted on. Taking a deep breath, Torrey rose. Clearly, she was seeing the old Holt from before. The time to clean her glasses, not literally, had come. She'd been ready to accuse him of seeing her with old thoughts and eyes. Instead, she was guilty as charged. Okay, how did she make the transition? Shift gears to seeing the new Holt. And understand and accept his changes. She groaned as one thought flooded her mind. More talk. Communicate, communicate, and do it again. Could they get enough said to clear the air and allow them to move forward?

She tossed the towels and robe into the dryer. As she set the dial, Torrey noted the cycle's length. They had an hour before the buzzer sounded.

Holt moved the wingback armchair closer to the sofa. He wanted to give Torrey the room and space she needed to feel comfortable in continuing their discussion. Easing her into giving him some history over the past two years might work better if she felt less cornered and put on the spot. Damn, he wanted to pat himself on the back for that. Some of his sister's lectures on modern women had gotten through versus the ones his mother and Stuart's Grandma Getty drilled into him. Holt grinned, rubbed his hands together, and sat knowing his work was cut out for him. He enjoyed research, especially the question-and-answer type. Could he keep his client-interviewing habits under wraps?

Torrey's footsteps sounded down the hall as he settled into the chair. Siam slept on top of his cat perch. His tail curled around him, almost hiding his nose and eyes. Mischa and Doxie lay side by side on their oversized dog bed. Neither moved as Torrey entered the room.

"Sorry for the outburst," she said, making her way to the sofa.

Holt waited until she sat down before replying. "With all that's happened, don't worry. I probably would have done the same."

Torrey placed a pillow behind her back, pulled her knees to her, and placed her feet on the sofa. "Thanks for clearing the table. I noticed as I came through the kitchen."

Holt waved his hand. "No problem. I helped make the mess. Least I can do is clean up."

Torrey leaned back, stretching her legs out in front of her. "Before we go further, I want to apologize for my attitude."

She glanced at Holt before continuing. His gaze rested on her. Good, she had his attention. "Two years doesn't seem much when you're busy living it and doing things life requires."

Holt's quick nod reassured her he listened to what she said. "I've got some questions, and I'm sure you do."

"Yes, I do. How about we give each other the high points we feel like immediately sharing? Then we talk about what went wrong this morning with the door incident?" Holt's smile and "sure" set off jitters in Torrey's stomach.

Their last date before she'd moved ended with them bickering harshly. The few e-mails they exchanged in an attempt to patch up that squabble hadn't helped. As the months rolled by, their exchanges and even phone chats lessened in frequency and duration. Could they get past the door incident and communicate? Torrey wondered how much of her own trepidations came from her insecurity and not from Holt.

"I'll go first since I suggested it. Moving out of state made sense since I needed work experience before heading to graduate school as I planned. Six months in New Mexico and Arizona turned into an offer to manage a retail chain store. I took the job without realizing how much I detest working for others." Somehow admitting aloud one of her pet peeves she never shared with Holt before felt scary. Why did his opinion matter? She inhaled, glanced at Holt, and exhaled. Quiet reigned between them as though each agreed to keep silent for a period of time.

Holt cleared his throat and leaned forward. "I'm going to jump in here. I graduated a year before you. I hung around campus taking graduate courses before I decided I needed to get a full-time job. I worked a few throwaway positions before you moved."

Holt rose and moved to the sofa. "Before either of us goes further, I want to talk about the door incident."

Torrey's face went white as her eyes widened. A light blush started along her cheeks and spread to her neck. Holt pried her fingers loose from her tightly folded hands resting on her knees. He took her hand in his. He raised her hand to his lips. He rubbed his cheek back and forth until he heard her shuddered sigh. He raised his head, held Torrey's gaze, and spoke. "What upset you? I can't fix..."

Torrey yanked her hand from his. She shot off the sofa. "You don't need to fix a thing," she exclaimed. Pacing as she continued, Torrey let her angst out. "I wish men understood we like our independence, too. We're just as capable as they are in many ways. You demeaned me in one way and in another you acted like you owned me."

As she turned, Holt draped his arm along the back of the sofa. Torrey's eyes narrowed as he sat there. His nod did nothing. He neither confirmed nor denied his actions. Blast, how could she argue with him if he didn't respond? Or was she itching to argue because that had been their prior style? Unsure of which fueled her, she spoke the one question bothering her since then. "Why did you do it?"

She flounced to the chair and dropped in it. She gripped the armrest and glared back at him, wanting to smack the bemused look off his face. Hitting Holt hadn't even entered her mind before. She knew she couldn't physically hurt him. Still, his smirking smile ignited more ire and agitation than she cared to admit.

"I'll answer when you tell me which part you're talking about." Holt faced her, resting his hands on his knees. "I want to understand, so I can—"

Torrey started to rise, her hands in the air.

Holt blurted out the rest of his thought before she stood. "So I can correct my mistakes."

Torrey dropped back into her chair. Her lips moved. Nothing came out. She blinked as her mouth hung open. She closed her mouth and shrugged.

Holt shook his head. "I know. I know. A shock, eh?"

Torrey nodded and watched him. Holt went on offering his defense. "I protect those I care about. You're one of them. Gwen's accused me of being overly protective. Sorry. It's one of those male things I can't change."

He placed his hands, palms down, on the coffee table separating the space between the sofa and the chair. As he leaned further forward, Siam jumped on the table and sat nearby, curling his tail around his feet. Mischa and Doxie stirred on their bed but slept on.

"I felt your tiny shake when I touched your hip." Holt reached over and petted Siam. Holt sat back and waited. He knew Torrey needed time to gather her next thoughts. Her arched eyebrow and tight lips said she heard him, but whether she accepted his defense or not wasn't clear.

Chills ran down his back the longer Torrey remained quiet. The last time he'd seen her this pensive, she hadn't spoken for ten minutes. All she told him then was to fuck off and walked out on him. His actions then deserved such a reply. Today his didn't. He hoped they didn't.

Each second ticked by, marked by the sounds of the mantel clock. Tick...tick...tick. Holt looked down. His heart sunk lower as more chills swept over him. Had he lost out before he even stood a chance?

"Torrey, can you..."

Torrey waved her hand and stood.

"I wish I didn't feel overwhelmed when you show you care." Torrey smoothed her hair with her hands. She turned to face Holt. "I'm not used to having someone around in that way."

Holt held his out to her. "I wanted to ask if you can forgive me. Your admission tells me you're bothered by your reaction as well. Is there a compromise? Somewhere in between where we both can be comfortable?"

Torrey backed up a couple of steps. She needed space to think. Too much was happening for her to be sure what mattered and what didn't. From somewhere in the kitchen, an obnoxious buzzing and beeping started growing in volume with each sound.

Holt rose, sighing and shaking his head. "Blasted cell phone."

Torrey smiled and followed him as he made his way into the kitchen. A loud chirp sounded with a buzz similar to an alarm clock. "That's mine."

She reached for her purse still hung over the back of a chair where she'd left it last night. The buzz echoed down the hall, louder this time. Torrey grabbed her purse strap and trotted down the hall. "I'll get the stuff out of the dryer. Be back in a few."

Holt rummaged in his gym bag until he found his phone. Caller ID showed Stuart's name and number. Great, what could he want? Holt thought twice about letting the call roll over to voice mail. Stuart wouldn't just leave a message and wait to hear back. Nope, he'd keep calling until he reached Holt. Holt rolled his eyes. Their friendship remained strong regardless of fights, distance, along with good or bad things happening in their lives. He knew he'd do the same thing if he didn't know where Stuart was. Truth was he didn't.

Holt hit the talk button. "Hey, Stuart!" Holt pulled the phone away from his ear as Stuart let loose a slew of cuss words. As Stuart's volume died down along with his cussing, Holt put the phone back to his ear.

"Look, man, you knew the storm hit with a vengeance. Torrey and I barely made it to her place without shit happening. Stop cursing like I owe you an explanation. 'Sides, this is the first my phone rang since yesterday. Reception evidently just returned."

Stuart rambled on for a few more moments before Holt interrupted him. "You're where? Vegas? What the hell are you doing there, dude?"

Holt looked around, making sure Torrey hadn't come back and heard his outburst. He didn't need her thinking he turned off his lawyer demeanor with Stuart and not her. Wait, he hadn't told her yet about law school and passing the bar. Pulling out the chair close to him, Holt sat down as he listened to Stuart's story.

"Joanna and I decided we hadn't had a vacation together for a while. We checked our credit cards and said what the heck. As we approached the airport, the only place we both hadn't been was Vegas. By the way, we're getting hitched."

Holt almost dropped his phone. "You're what?"

Stuart explained how he proposed on the flight and Joanna said yes. "Question now, man, is can you and Torrey get here for it?"

"Sorry, bro. No can do. We're stranded at her place until the flood waters recede. Hug Joanna for me and we'll celebrate when you get back." Holt scooted forward on the chair and leaned out hoping to catch a glimpse of Torrey as she made her way back down the hall.

Torrey waved as she exited the guestroom. Towels hung over her arm along with her bathrobe. She held her phone to her ear, talking as she turned toward her bedroom. Holt caught part of her conversation. "You told Stuart *yes*?"

Chapter Sixteen

Torrey tossed the dry towels and her bathrobe on her bed. She sat as she ended her call with Joanna. The last person Torrey expected to get married was doing just that. Where did that leave her? Single and unattached? Alone and...whatever it all meant, she knew one thing. Holt waited for her back in the kitchen. His actions weren't tawdry or shallow. Neither of them had run at the first ripple of anger. Just maybe there was more to him than she remembered. The time to explore things more had come.

Torrey quickly folded the towels. As she hung up her bathrobe, she noticed Holt's clothes on the floor. His sneakers needed separate washing. Mud and dirt caked the tops and sides. They needed rinsing out before she dared put them in the washer. Humming as she gathered the rest of a partial load out of her hamper, she noticed the sleeve sticking out from the rest of the clothes in the closet. She swallowed hard as she reached for the item. He found the shirt she saved and occasionally wore. Would he ask about it? Did she need to volunteer the information?

"Hey, Torrey," Holt called out.

"Yes?"

"You going to be much longer? My stomach is growling again. I can make us some sandwiches and more coffee." Holt's offer of food sounded good. Even though only three hours had passed since breakfast, their midmorning snack needed augmentation. Torrey didn't remember eating much at dinner. Butterflies in her stomach and seeing the one man she kept comparing others against left her no appetite. Now she was ravenous, and even though she wanted to say no, her growling stomach vetoed the notion. "Sure, go ahead. No more coffee for me. I'll be there in a moment. Do you have other clothes to add to this load?"

"Everything is in the bedroom. Need help?"

Torrey smiled, unable to help herself. Every time Holt offered assistance or partnered in some way, she recognized why she distanced herself from the other dates and men she'd tried seeing. Torrey giggled as Grandma Getty's voice came to mind. Memories of her lecturing each of them—Stuart, Holt, and her—after they'd fought about friends and marrying the person meant for them flashed across her mind. Grandma Getty focused on her and Holt in particular. Torrey shook her head as she closed the washer's lid. Had she missed the obvious back then?

"No, I'm good," Torrey called as she made her way back down the hall.

Holt glanced over his shoulder as Torrey entered the kitchen, humming. "Food will be ready in a moment. Sit while I finish up."

Torrey paused near him. Several thoughts appeared to preoccupy her. Her pursued lips and distant gaze said her thoughts were elsewhere. Holt inhaled and held his breath. Torrey's fresh scent enveloped him in ways he wished happened daily. She wore lightly scented lotion and minimal makeup. Her natural appearance and appeal attracted him more than he realized. Women who wore more makeup or stronger scents didn't upset him. He found heady perfumes cloying and distracting along with heavy makeup, too. More often than not, his clients needed instructions on what to wear to court and why. Gwen had taken to having him talk about professional clothing, appearance, and why this was important in the courtroom to many of the shelter's residents.

"Who was your call from?" Holt dried his hands and approached Torrey. She faced him, her lips still puckered as though she lingered in thought. He leaned down and kissed her.

Torrey startled as Holt pressed his lips to hers. "Ooh," she gasped, jumping back. She blinked, inhaled sharply, and tilted her head back. Holt's worried gaze greeted her. "I'm okay. Lost in thought."

Holt nodded. "No problem. Stuart called. I wondered if Joanna called you."

"Yes, and I'm still stuck at how fast they decided to get married." Torrey set plates next to the sandwiches on the cutting board Holt used.

"Caught me by surprise. Yet, not too fast either. They've dated off and on for a year before seeing each other steadily for the last six months." Holt filled two glasses with water and handed them to Torrey. "Take these to the table. I'll get plates and utensils."

Torrey set the glasses on the table. "I think I understand why I get upset when you try to protect me."

"Oh?" Holt's tone didn't chill her intention on getting out what bothered her and what she needed to do about it.

"Yes, I've been on my own, doing for myself, without having to take too many others into account. Only Joanna, our staff, my limited community boards I serve on. Gwen is the one person who I've confided in from time to time on small things. I've missed having a best friend to talk to."

Holt set a plate in front of her. "I get where you're coming from. Stuart's great for guy things. It's hard asking your sister about women issues."

Torrey snorted. "What women issues? You had them falling all over you, last I remember."

Holt debated how to answer Torrey. "Well," he started as he sat down. "That was two years ago. A lot happened since then. Care to share more? Or is it my turn?"

He waited for Torrey to answer; instead she stayed quiet. "Guess it's my turn, then. Right after you moved, I finished my last internship. This one was with a law firm. The senior partner offered me a full time job as a law clerk with one condition. I returned to grad school and finished my master's. After discussing the matter with the other partners, they were willing to pay for law school, too."

"Wow, I hope you took them up on the offer." Torrey bit into her sandwich and chewed.

Holt sipped his water, and continued. "Yes, I did. I passed the bar a year and a half later. I went to school nights and summers, taking as many courses as I could without hurting my B-plus average. I opened my own practice in January."

Torrey applauded. "Great for you. I got a similar offer except it came from an older cousin who didn't have heirs. She never married or adopted. She wanted me to be able to succeed on my own and 'know the value of a buck,' to quote her. I couldn't touch more than a set amount for school each year. When her health declined right after I finished my undergrad studies, I moved to care for her and got the jobs I mentioned earlier. She died unexpectedly, leaving me the option of moving back here or going to school in Arizona."

"Gwen didn't mention that part when she told me you moved back." Holt finished half of his sandwich and drank more water before wiping his mouth. "Go on, please, I interrupted you."

"I decided sitting in a classroom didn't suit me. I got my master's online through Cal State San Francisco. Joanna and I opened Ladies' Satisfaction around the same time I started classes. I gained enough business experience to test out of many of the required classes for a business administration concentration. The results made sense, given I owned a business and the classes left interested me." Torrey finished her sandwich.

Holt drank the rest of his water. "I wash you dry?" he offered as he rose.

"You rinse. I put in the dishwasher. We let it do the washing." Torrey crumpled her napkin, placing on it her plate, before she pushed it away.

"I've been thinking about you're feeling overwhelmed. Maybe the issue for each of us is we're seeing the old us. As much as we feel comfortable in the known, the new offers potential we've yet to explore." Holt filled his glass partway and drank it. "More water?"

"No, thank you." Torrey walked over to the sink. She opened the dishwasher and started filling it.

Holt rinsed the rest of their dishes and handed them to Torrey. "Is being independent important to you?" He leaned over, brushed his lips over her cheek. "I'm sorry I didn't explain before I nudged you aside with the door. I surmised you needed help when asking would have worked better."

Torrey glanced at him. Her flushed cheeks indicated she toyed with what he was saying. Each time she met his gaze head-on, she blinked and quickly looked away. Holt dried his hands. "I can see something is bothering you. I need you to tell me straight what it is."

Torrey caught her top lip between her teeth, worrying it. She opened her mouth to speak, shook her head, and closed her mouth.

Holt cupped her cheek as he spoke. "Torrey, nothing you say or feel is wrong with me. I can't read your mind. I erred earlier. Talk to me please so I can begin to understand and not make the same mistake in the future."

"How do I explain..." Torrey paused, sighed, and closed her eyes. She knuckled a lone tear off her cheek. Pain flooded through her. Not physical pain. Deep emotional hurt that she thought she healed when she moved on to her next relationship. Torrey tried to inhale. Instead, a shuddered watery sigh came out. Blinking, she tried to avoid looking at Holt. Even evade the confused concerned eyes watching her and the soft smile warming his face at the same time. Unable to hold back, she buried her face in her hands and gave in to the tears.

Warmth surrounded her and strong arms lifted her up. "It's okay," Holt whispered against her hair.

Torrey tried to sniffle and regain control. No such luck. The damn floodgates refused to close. Torrent upon torrent of pent-up angst, anguish, and fear, along with hurt, over churned their individual barriers. One by one, each flushed out anything in their path.

Holt's breath blew across her cheek. He shifted her in his arms. "Come on, sweetie. I've got you. I'm here."

Torrey fumbled with her shirt, trying to wipe her eyes. A soft cloth brushed her leg. "Reach down with your right hand. I can't hand it up higher to you and still carry you into the bedroom."

Torrey grabbed the cloth, scrubbed at the tears streaming down her face, and wiped the ones blurring her vision. She gasped as Holt slowly sank down on the bed.

Holt held Torrey closer. He rested his head atop hers. What had set her off? He knew better than to pry. Comforting her mattered more.

"Torrey," Holt began, rocking gently back and forth. "Can you share? What's upset you?"

Torrey's muffled sniffles told him she wanted quiet for now. He held her, rocking and humming the lullaby his mother put him to sleep with as a child.

Torrey huddled tighter to Holt. Lord, the months of loneliness and endless hours of wondering if she made the right decision. Here now in Holt's arms combined with their earlier lovemaking confirmed she did the best she could. Somewhere in the last two years, she knew she wanted more. The long-term connection and passion mattered now. She wanted love and companionship mixed with her lover's connection to her. How did she explain tears of joy mingled with tears of pain leading to release and relief simultaneously?

She gulped air as she raised her face from Holt's chest. She smiled at the huge wet spot spreading across the front of the faded shirt he wore. Somehow letting that shirt go with the donations didn't feel right as she considered the idea. Sighing heavily, she rubbed cloth she held over her face. Thank goodness, Holt had pulled one of the plush washcloths from the stack in the bathroom. She wouldn't have little pieces of tissue sticking to her face.

"Holt," she whispered, clearing her throat. "I'm okay," she stated in a calmer, firmer voice.

"Are you sure?" Holt's warm breath fanned over her cheek and ear as he leaned back.

Torrey nodded, trying to smile as she worked to regain more composure. There was no easy way to describe what she felt. Talking about it might help get her emotions out in a way she needed rather than keeping them tightly reined in any longer.

"Do you remember our last date? The few weeks we spent together more as a couple than friends with benefits?" She leaned back into Holt's arm that remained around her. His touch and closeness triggered a sense of calm and rightness in being here like this now. Torrey hoped she could say in words what her heart and gut fought over.

"Yes. That was right before I started seeing Nancy. Then I moved on, thinking you didn't want me around. You acted standoffish next time I saw you."

"You're right. I took your interest in Nancy way too personally." Holt opened his mouth to reply. Torrey pressed her fingers on his lips. "Wait a moment, please."

Holt's tongue slid hotly along her parted fingers until he suckled two. His soft "yes" came out almost indiscernible, given how preoccupied he was. Torrey giggled and slowly withdrew her fingers. She shook one at him. "Behave while I go on."

"Okay for now." Holt's wink exploded more than warm feelings deep in her. Desire flared up, ready to pull her down into its sumptuous lure. She inhaled sharply, arching her eyebrows, as her eyes widened. There was no denying how much Holt turned her on. Before she gave into the heady need, her libido wished to dance with, she needed to finish what she started.

Chapter Seventeen

"What I didn't realize until after you showed interest in Nancy was how attached I became to you. No matter how hard I tried to shake my feelings, nothing worked. I'd fallen for you. Somewhere, somehow, we became more than friends." Torrey's voice faded off.

Holt nuzzled Torrey's neck. He felt the warmth grow as he kissed her cheek. By the time he reached her ear as he placed small kisses mixed with nips along her jawline, she blasted heat stronger than he anticipated. Pulling back, he noticed the flush covering her neck and cheeks.

"Is that why you kept the shirt I loaned you that night? Why you kept your distance?" There, he voiced the two questions nagging him since he had found his shirt in her closet. Would she give him the straight on it or dodge answering him altogether?

With her in his arms, he could feel every breath she took. And if he focused, even the little movements she made as he spoke. Her sudden sharp breath as he mentioned the shirt caught his acute attention. Did she think he wasn't paying attention?

Torrey squirmed and leaned away from him. Hmmm, he'd touched on an apparently sensitive issue. No way was she putting up shields again. Holt slid Torrey off his lap and pushed her back onto the pillows behind her.

Torrey gasped as she landed on the pillows. Holt hovered above her, grinning. He kept himself off her by leaning on one arm. She moved her lips. No words came out. Holt lowered himself until inches separated them. "I'm gonna say this once so there's no confusion. I want the truth. I need to know what's going on in your heart, head, and gut. That's important to me. Not what you think I want to hear."

Torrey swallowed any smart-ass retort her ego wanted to throw at Holt. She blinked, inhaled, followed by a slow exhale that brought her breasts within heartbeats of Holt's chest. She could feel every piece of her face scanned by his gaze. The man read her without training. He could then and still could now. Except...something was different. What was it? Torrey couldn't pinpoint it. Vaguely though, it was as if he listened and took in everything she said. She bet if she asked he could summarize their conversation almost word for word.

"Yes, I kept your shirt. Each time I wore it, I got to keep a piece of you to myself. It was as if your arms wrapped around me every time I put it on. I didn't wash it for months because your scent stayed on it. If I longed for you, I buried my face in the shirt and inhaled. I finally laundered it, hoping to break the longing and angst I felt long after you disappeared from campus." Torrey blew out a pent-up, angst-filled sigh. Her chest brushed against Holt's and fell.

Holt's throaty "uh-huh" kept her eyes on him. He rolled to her side, pushing a pillow from his side of the bed under his head. He jostled the mattress some as he settled in beside her. "Go on if there's more. I didn't know this. Of course, I couldn't, because I wasn't there."

"There's not much more to say except this. Yes, I stayed away due to Nancy. Most women don't understand men having women friends. I didn't want to tone down our connection either. I tried thinking of ways I could continue being friends without possibly harming your relationship with Nancy." Torrey paused, inhaled, and continued. "And at the same time, I knew I couldn't go on seeing you with her, feeling the way I did. I cut the ties and broke things off. I've learned more about this since I opened the store. I never realized how much I felt in competition with Nancy and the others you commented on until I heard it from other women."

"I wish women could understand why guys look. I know I'll keep looking until the day I die. But—and that's the key word—I'm not hunting for someone else when and if I do. Window-shopping is nice. Eye candy is nice. It can and does spice up home, so I am told."

Torrey glanced at Holt. He lay on his back with his arms tucked behind his head. She wanted to punch him for his last remarks. Problem was, he was right. She would keep looking, too. Not to find others, but to see what was out there. After all, chemistry didn't have a conscience to keep it under control. She smiled, reached up with her hand, and tweaked his nose.

Holt quickly turned toward Torrey. "What was that for?"

Her impish grin and shrug told him he had better be careful what he said off-the-cuff. She puckered her lips, raised her hand again, and...

Holt didn't wait. He thrust his hand into her hair and pulled her to him. His lips captured hers. He wanted her as hotly now as he had the moment he'd caught her reflection in the bar's mirror. Images of a cartoon character with steam blowing out his ears popped into his mind. Holt tried to keep his mirth at bay. No such luck. He broke off their French kiss as he burst out laughing. Tossing his head back, he howled with laughter.

Torrey's rustling and stilted movements calmed him. "Sorry, darlin'. We're steaming things up. Unfortunately, my ironical sense of humor kicked up with a hoot of an image. The cartoon character we used to keep on our laptops for the times we were ready to blow due to stress, class load, and general angst."

Torrey clapped her hand over her mouth as the image Holt talked about came to mind. She snorted, chortled behind her hand, choked, and started coughing. She drew her hand away, fanning herself. "I'm all right," she managed to rasp out in between breaths. "Gosh, that cartoon got us into more trouble with that poli-sci class than we ever imagined. Thanks for reminding me."

"You're welcome," Holt murmured, his voice caressing her ear and neck. "Where were we? Oh yes, doing this." One hand cupped her chin. His other retangled in her hair. He brushed his lips over hers before renewing their French kiss.

His tongue curled around hers. Hints of their coffee laced with smatters of jam and cinnamon tweaked her taste buds. Masculine scents of sweat and deodorant wafted past her nose each time she inhaled.

Beard stubble greeted her fingers as she stroked Holt's cheek. As her hand roved higher, she encountered his soft curls. Some men would complain about their curly hair. Holt never did. He accepted things in ways that flattered him. She hadn't realized this until now. Threading her hand more into his soft locks, Torrey deepened their kiss.

Holt pressed more fully against her. His hand stroked along the edge of her shorts waistband. She sucked in her stomach, allowing his hand to bunch up part of her top on his next pass.

"Hmm," Holt crooned, easing off their kiss. "You're warm all over. How about we lose some of these clothes?"

He tugged the material bunched in his hand, trying to work her top higher. Torrey slid her hands down Holt's neck, enjoying the heat she felt from him as well. As much as she enjoyed making out with him, getting him nude was better. Much better, if it led to mind-blowing orgasms as before.

Torrey pushed against Holt, trying to sit up. "I'm shucking. How about you?" Torrey began working her top up over her breasts as she continued trying to push herself upright. Holt's hand covered hers.

"How about you let me undress you?" His wink and airborne kiss melted any ideas of doing things herself.

Torrey dropped her hands to her sides. "Ooh, yes," she enthusiastically agreed. "I think sitting up or standing would be easier. Much easier on the clothes and both of us."

Torrey sat up and scooted across the bed. She left her top where it lay, leaving one breast exposed with the rest bunched up under her other. She struck the most provocative pose she knew. One leg and knee slightly in front of the other, her hands on her hips and shaking her ass.

Holt couldn't contain his laughter. He tried to sit up. Torrey turned around and bent over, shaking her ass more as she hummed an off-key tune.

"Stop. Pll—eease stop," Holt stammered in between fits of laughter. "Whoever told you those moves were sexy?"

Torrey turned around, put her hands on her hips, and stuck her tongue out at Holt. "You did, silly goose. The time you were trying to teach me how to walk in two-inch heels."

"I did not."

"Did too." Torrey shook her hips and ass again. "You even tried on a pair of my roommate's heels in an attempt to show me how Gwen walked in them."

"Oh shit! Now I remember!" Holt covered his face with his hands. He peeked through his fingers at Torrey. "And I landed smack on my ass as your roommate and Stuart came through the door. My bruised ass and ego spent the better part of the next semester living that down."

"Yes, I remember Stuart getting you a pair of hot-pink three-inch heels as a birthday gift." Torrey stopped dancing around to the tune she'd been humming. "Now where were we?"

Holt rolled across the bed, his feet touched the floor, and he stood. He took long strides, closing the space separating him and Torrey. As he reached her, he reached out, taking the hem of her top and tugging it upward. "Here is where we are. And this is coming off. *Now.*"

Holt didn't wait for Torrey's reaction to his emphasis on "now." He pulled the material from beneath her breast, easing it up quickly until both his hands were at the same level. His gaze met hers. He remembered one of Torrey's favorite fantasies. A little dominant foreplay got her hot and steamy. A scene formed as he caught Torrey's arms behind her after working her top over her head and partway down her arms.

"How about we play a game?" Holt nipped Torrey's neck, worrying the flesh with his teeth. "I strip you and you do what I say?"

Torrey's humming ceased. Holt didn't bother with acknowledging this. He knew she contemplated what he said. He gently turned her around so she faced the mirror atop her dresser. "Actions speak louder than words. Are you in?"

He reached over Torrey's shoulder, sliding his hand down her bra and into the cup. He palmed the underside of her breast, stroking her semi-hard nipple with his thumb as he spoke again. "Shall I stop? Ah, these are so delicious." Holt stroked Torrey's nipple again. He leaned forward and nipped her shoulder. "A yes is all I need to go on. Make that a 'yes, sir' and you'll get a whole lot more."

Torrey tried to swallow. Neither her dry mouth nor throat allowed her the vocal response she wanted to give. Holt's hot breath singed her neck as he spoke. His husky whisper scalded its way across her shoulder, singed her collarbone, and streaked its way deep inside her ear and libido. Goose bumps ran up and down her arms as Holt stroked closer to her aching nipple. She looked up. His eyes met hers in the mirror.

He arched an eyebrow, began removing his hand, and shrugged. Torrey shook her head no and stomped her foot. Holt cocked his head, left his hand partway inside her bra cup, and blew in her ear. Torrey willed her eyes to stay open. Strong sensations warped through her. Holt's breathing turned her on more than she realized. Torrey squinted as desire swept her up in its heady hold. She caught Holt's unspoken question. She nodded vigorously twice. Her eyes closed, and she sagged back against him.

"Good, I see you figured out how to make your wants known. Here's your task, my lovely. For each piece of clothing I remove from you, you must remove like from me. Each caress and touch, every kiss and fondle, you are to repeat. Do you understand?"

Torrey gulped, hoping her voice returned soon. All she could do was nod and smile. Undressing Holt tit-for-tat would be interesting. Neither of them wore much. Touch for touch, kiss for kiss, fondle for fondle…Torrey inhaled sharply as Holt pulled her top off her other arm and tossed it on the bed.

"Now *your* turn," he stated, drawing out "your." Holt pulled his hands out of her bra and stepped away from her. Torrey swallowed, grateful her mouth and throat were no longer dry. She licked her lips, opened her eyes, and located Holt as she glanced in the mirror.

Holt sidestepped and eased his way around her. He didn't stop until he faced her. He stood close to her with his arms and hands at his side. He watched her. Torrey swore he almost challenged her with the look of determination in his eyes.

"Raise your arms please, sir." Torrey advanced toward Holt, her palms facing outward. As she reached him, she eased her hands along his exposed skin left bare from him lifting his arms.

"Woman, your hands are warm." Holt sucked in his stomach and held his breath. "How do you plan to get the shirt over my head and down my arms?"

Torrey arched an eyebrow, squinting as she sized up the situation before her. She looked down to where her hands barely met as they touched Holt's stomach, then up to his cheeky grin and twinkling eyes, and higher to where his hands and arms reached over his head. She puckered her mouth then caught her bottom lip between her teeth, closed one eye, and sized up her situation again. She pulled back one of her hands and...

"Crap," Holt yelled, landing hard on the mattress. Torrey didn't wait. Instead, she lunged for him.

Holt tried to roll to his side. Torrey grabbed his arm, calling out. "Foul, sir. Foul!"

Holt rolled back toward her. Torrey quickly straddled his waist, shoving her hands underneath his shirt. She found his nipples, plucking them between her nails, twisting his small bits of skin like he had hers. Torrey released them. Slowly she dragged her fingertips over and around his engorged sensitive skin.

"How am I doing, *sir*?" Torrey asked, squirming tighter to Holt each time he jerked or grunted.

"Keep that up and I'm gonna—" Holt gasped as Torrey ground her pelvis hotly against him.

"Coming with your clothes on, *sir*, isn't as appeasing as without." Torrey yelped as Holt gripped her hips.

"Enough, you sassy tart." Holt grinned, brushed his lips over hers, and rolled them on their sides, their legs tangled together.

Torrey's giggles brushed over Holt's ear and fanned down his neck. He slid his arms slowly up her torso, tickling and tweaking exposed flesh until he reached her waist. Pulling her to him, He caught Torrey's earlobe with his lips. Her muffled vocals indicated she was as turned on as him. Could he get her to slow down enough to let each of them strip off the rest of their clothes on their own? The jeans he wore had next to no room for his balls. If his cock swelled much more, explaining pubic hair in the zipper to the poor gent who got the jeans would be next to impossible. The fly on his briefs threatened to let everything loose and not in a good way. Cheap knockoffs didn't always designate quality. Lots of pubic hair didn't help either.

Torrey's sizzling breath blew through his hair, warming his scalp and ear. She nipped and licked her way to his jaw. Holt sucked in air as she wormed her hand between them. Metal clicked as she undid his belt. Soon that got tossed to the side, off the bed, landing on the floor. Next, he felt her fingers fumble with the waistband button of his jeans. Great, he had to act now or she'd have him undressed before she was. Temptress knew how to egg him on. She might not remember what got him harder or prolonged things, but she knew what spots and touches punched his desire to a new level.

"S–S–low down–n," he stammered as Torrey's hand slipped past the undone button and worked to get underneath the thick elastic waistband of his briefs. Holt tried to pull his leg from between Torrey's. The snugger they got to each other, the more the crotch of the blasted jeans crushed his balls to him. Another pull and either he'd have bruised nuts or the backside of the jeans would burst. He heard more thread popping and rips the more he moved.

"Why should I slow down?" Torrey glided away from him as Holt created space between them.

He inhaled, closed his eyes, quickly rattled off a silent five count, and reopened his eyes. "'Cuz I want you naked, sweetums. If we keep going at this rate, we will come with our clothes on, as you observed, or rip the hell out of our clothes trying to get them off. Either one wastes the mood and fuel we've generated."

Torrey's soft smile reached her eyes and grew the more she gave him one eye-humping gaze after another as her eyes roved up and down him. She rolled to the edge of the bed, stood, and announced her intentions. "On the count of three, we shuck clothes. One...two..."

Before Torrey could reach three, Holt stood and shoved his hands into his jeans and briefs. They hit the floor, pooling around his ankles. His cock jutted out from his groin.

Chapter Eighteen

Holt reached out with his free hand. "From the look you've got, I know what you want." He stepped forward, grasping her wrist and tugged.

Torrey fell forward, landing against Holt. "What you got in mind?"

Holt grazed his knuckles over Torrey's pubic hair. "Oh, this and that."

He quickly stroked her clit and coated his finger in her wetness. He circled her clit on his upward stroked, edging closer to her pouting pearl. Torrey's soft moan of pleasure told him he had her attention. Slowly, Holt worked his finger back and forth, just missing her clit. As Torrey's wetness grew, Holt slipped his arm around her waist, pulling her closer to him. His lips brushed over her shoulder before he nipped.

"Keep squirming, darlin'. You are so wet and delicious tasting, too, I bet." Holt freed his slicked finger from between Torrey's legs.

He shot Torrey a sideways glance. He moved sideways creating space between them. "Coming willingly or..."

"Oh, I'll come I'm sure. Whatever you have in mind, I'll be coming." Torrey interlaced her fingers with his. "Lead the way, sir. This obedient one will follow."

Holt bit his lip to keep from laughing. Torrey's wide eyes and exaggerated nod added to the hilarity of her being obedient only if it suited her. He slipped his hand free from hers. "Oh, love, you are a card. Just follow and we'll see what happens."

Torrey's breathy "sure" warmed his back as he moved toward the bed. He stopped as he reached the edge of the bed. Torrey's breasts softly touched him as she moved up behind him. He reached back, found her hand, and curled his around hers.

"Move around me, love." He nodded with his head. "On your hands and knees with your lovely ass facing away. A few swats would distract me too temptingly. I want to taste you."

"I want your taste, too. Salty, masculine, and *creamy*." Holt swore Torrey purred as she said creamy. He wanted to come, not in her mouth, rather deep inside her again as they rocked to another round of mind-dazzling orgasms.

Torrey scrambled on to the mattress, working her way across the bed. She turned around, facing him as he instructed. She raised her head. "Now what?" She grinned and tried to shake her ass. The bed shook and swayed a bit.

"Stop please before I lose my focus, you vixen!" Holt motioned with his hand. "Scoot back more until you're in the middle. I need room to lay back under you." Torrey's quick nod of understanding as she licked her lips gripped him more than he expected. Lord, how could he have forgotten how much Torrey enjoyed oral sex? He turned around and backed up to the mattress. He sat as the edge of it hit the backs of his knees. He lowered himself until he lay on his back looking up at a bemused Torrey.

"Need help?" she quipped. Holt shook his head, and arched his back to raise more of his lower torso underneath Torrey.

"Just a few more seconds and..." Torrey's soft giggle stopped his words. So she wanted to play. Play he would, and soon she'd get the prize she lusted after.

Holt slid up the bed more until he saw his prize, Torrey's swollen nether lips with her engorged clit peeking out. He snaked his hands out around her hips and pushed gently, lowering her to his mouth. Torrey's gasped "oh" and moans told him she liked the first swipe of his tongue over her. Puckering his lips, he suckled the gem he knew would send her bucking and squirming very soon.

Torrey closed her eyes as Holt's lips brushed her pubis. More wetness flooded her with each lap. The man knew how to keep her on the edge. Her eyes flew open as two fingers traced the opening of her vagina. Memories flashed of Holt's expertise in finding her G-spot and massaging it. Could she withstand his two-prong dose to bringing her off?

Torrey inhaled deeply, shuddering with each breath. Holt knew what brought a woman to the edge and pushed her over the edge into one simultaneous orgasm. Before he got her there, she wanted him thrusting in her mouth as he rolled closer to his own release. She lowered her head, opened her mouth, and engulfed him.

Holt's hips lifted off the bed. His muffled groans said she scored in more ways than he expected. His fingers lingered partway in her while his tongue scalded over and around her clit twice more.

Intermingling quick flicks of her tongue across his cockhead on her downward dip, Torrey bobbed her head up and down in quick succession. Each time she reached his balls, Holt jerked due to her tightening her lips and sucking in her cheeks. She released the suction on her upward stroke. She could tell she got to him more with each suckle and lick. Holt reached up and gripped her hips. His heavy breathing heated her mons as he gasped air. "Slow down. I wanted to bring you off and taste you. I forgot how good you are at giving head."

Torrey popped Holt out of her mouth, holding him with one hand. She smiled before she licked her lips. "What did you have in mind? I had a couple of blissful orgasms. If you want more, then I suggest we try a different approach."

Holt chortled. "I don't think I can last much more with you licking and sucking as hotly as you've been. While I'd loved to bring you off hard like this morning, I suspect each of us is more worn out than we'd like to admit."

"Giving up already?" Torrey started to rock back on her heels away from Holt.

"Hold on, please. How about some good old-fashioned spooning with intercourse combined?" Holt reached up and fondled Torrey's breasts. He scooted forward, captured each nipple in his mouth, sucked them, and let go. "I want to come together like we've done in the past if we can coordinate things."

Torrey sighed. A stiff yawn followed. She looked at the bedside clock. Two p.m. While it wasn't late on a normal day—what had been normal about yesterday or today?—they were both short on sleep and running on adrenaline from last night. A nap curled up in Holt's arms felt right and made sense. Falling asleep in a postcoital embrace sounded wonderful. Later on at dinner, she'd tell him what her newfound feelings were. She'd take a chance on saying out loud the three words she whispered two years ago each time she saw him and kept hidden in her heart ever since, *I love you.*

Holt eased out from under Torrey and stood. "Make yourself comfortable, lady. I'm ready to finish what we started. I want to come long and hard deep inside you."

Torrey rolled to her side. "Probably a pillow under my hip makes sense since you're taller than me. That way you can ease into me from behind and still play with me as you like."

Holt smiled and reached for the box of condoms sitting on the nightstand. "Neither of us is going to last long once I touch your clit. I know how wet you are." He tore open the foil packet, eased the condom on, and kneeled on the bed. "Ready if you are, my darling."

Torrey tried to vocalize her consent except her throat tightened on her, going dry from her mouth down to her vocal chords. All she could do was nod and smile. As she lay back on the pillows, she wondered how good Holt was at reading sign language. Not that she knew any. Maybe if she pointed, nodded, and smiled he might understand.

Holt watched as Torrey kept enthusiastically nodding. He inhaled to keep from snorting and laughing. He'd gotten to her so much that she couldn't speak. He wasn't going to miss an excellent opportunity. He reached out, capturing her nipples between his thumb and finger. He twisted and pulled like he'd done earlier, but this time he applied a bit more pressure all the way out to the edge of her erect nipples.

Torrey arched her shoulders, forcing her breasts forward. Holt caught the look of pleasure flooding her face before she closed her eyes and exhaled. He let go of her nipples and followed her down on to the bed, bracing himself on his elbows and forearms with their chests mere inches apart. He matched his breathing with Torrey's. It was as if they were one in actions, thought, and focus. They lacked the last intimate physical connection, him deep within Torrey, rocking them to whatever number of mind-blowing orgasms they could reach before sleep overwhelmed them.

Torrey gently fondled him until his eyes met hers. She licked her lips and glanced at her hand. Holt gulped air as she tightened her hold on him. "Easy, darlin'. Much more of that and I'll come."

Holt rolled to his side as Torrey let go. "Come on top and ride us to the crest and back, love."

Torrey swallowed hard and smiled. "Yes," she managed to get out, despite her hoarseness.

Holding Holt with one hand, she used her other to steady herself as she straddled him. Moments later, she guided him deep within her. Holt placed his hands on her hips, stabilizing her jerky movements. "You set the pace," he groaned on her next downward plunge.

She sucked in air as Holt rose to meet her. He held her steady barely moving his hips as he thrust rapidly in and out of her, stroking the fire waiting to explode deep in her belly. One last lunge deep within her and he fell back, breathing hard. "You are so wet," he groaned. Holt's hands dropped to his sides. "Baby, I don't know how much more you can take. I'm ready to explode."

She ground tight against Holt, leaving no space between them as she began short jerks of her hips, mimicking what he'd done to her minutes before. "You said set the pace. I'm gonna enjoy the ride for a bit longer." Holt groaned deep in his throat as she tightened around him. The look on his face along with his short breaths said she had him right where she wanted him, hard, skirting the edge of a strong orgasm, and deep inside her.

Torrey picked up speed as her own need grew. Twice before at Holt's encouragement, she'd ridden him. Both times, their mutual orgasms sent them both out of their bodies and into a space where nothing but being there together mattered. Of course, mind-blowing orgasms happened with others, but nothing compared to the aftercare that she and Holt lavished on each other. Torrey sucked in her stomach as tight as she could and milked Holt using the Kegel exercises she recently learned. The healthcare team at the shelter was right! Ripples set off more ripples and in turn created a stimulation that had Torrey panting along with Holt.

Holt captured his bottom lip between his teeth and inhaled sharply. When had the minx learned this trick? Betwixt the need to come and the urge to roll Torrey on her back while plunging into her balls-deep at a faster rate, he knew he couldn't take away from her the enjoyment her lead was giving her.

"Ahhh, woman. You're so friggin' tight. Keep milking me like that and I'm gonna..." His balls tightened against him. His cock stiffened. Deep in his belly, shudders began as white lights flashed behind his slammed-shut eyelids. "Come," he shouted as the first spurt of jism shot out of him, soaking the inside of the condom.

Torrey caught her breath in gasps as Holt's hands found her hips, keeping her in pace as he matched her thrust for thrust. It was as though neither of them moved far from the other. Midway on his next thrust, Torrey gulped and held her breath. Wave after wave of hot desire swelled up deep in her and rocketed out to crash back over her as one intense orgasm after another bombarded her. Her clit pulsed and throbbed with each stroke of Holt's shorter jerks. He let go of her hip with one hand and found her clit with his thumb.

"Yesss," Torrey managed to get out before she gave into the tsunami-size orgasm claiming her.

Holt knew the moment Torrey gave herself over to the bliss roaring through her. He felt her go slack and begin to slump over him as she continued to spasm around him. He gritted his teeth as another burst of need grabbed him and propelled him toward his second climax.

His eyes slammed shut as one last spurt of semen rose from deep in his balls, up his cock, and spattered down and over him. He arched his neck as his head dropped back. Holt tried to suck in air as his mouth opened. Instead, deep moans and sighs roared out of him. He swore his toes curled as one spasm after another whipped up and down his body. Torrey's limp sighs and soft vocals reached through the fog steadily growing in his mind. Using his hands, working by touch alone since his eyes refused to open; he found Torrey's arms and eased her to his side. He didn't know how they remained joined. He didn't care either. Sleep demanded a response. An affirmative response both of them wanted and needed.

Holt forced his heavy eyelids open. The room blurred around him. He made out the larger items close by. He worked two pillows beneath Torrey's head before he cradled her on his shoulder. Reaching behind him, he tugged and pulled what covers he could reach over them. Reassured Torrey was okay and spooned to him, Holt eased a pillow out from under her head and beneath his. He took a deep breath, exhaled, and let sleep claim him.

Chapter Nineteen

"Achoo!" Holt reached up, rubbed his nose, and sneezed again. His hand scrubbed over his face until something brushed over it. He raised his hand, shaking it at the same time. He shook his head and cracked one eye open. He blinked hard. Why couldn't he see? Had they slept that long?

A muffled plaintiff meow sounded as Holt's hand rubbed his nose more, pushing on the item lying on his face. His hand closed around the object. He lifted his fingers and opened both eyes. "Siam," he complained softly. "Get your tail and carcass off my pillow, please."

Siam's answer of two more tail thumps on his face and head brought him to full awareness. He slowly turned his head in the direction of where he remembered Torrey lying as they fell asleep. She wasn't there. Had Siam woken both of them up? Or had she risen and left him sleeping? He wanted to talk to her about pieces of their earlier discussion.

Holt turned his head toward the window, hoping to get an idea of how long he'd slept. On her side with her hand tucked under her cheek, Torrey slept. A smile graced her lips. Holt let his gaze rove over her snuggled under the sheets and blankets, blissfully snoozing. Curled up close by her, Mischa and Doxie slept. Holt rolled to his side, lifting his head to avoid hitting Siam. The blasted cat glared at him as if he expected him to stay put to continue to warm his feline arse with the heat escaping his head.

"Look, you ditzy cat." Holt reached out and stroked him as he sat up. "My head is not your warming spot, okay?" He smiled at Siam's toothy hiss and glare. He ruffled Siam's fur twice more. "Now you have reason to be upset."

Holt glanced at the clock on the nightstand. Five p.m. He'd slept two hours. Had Torrey gotten up and come back to bed? He didn't want to wake her. Their sleep the night before was broken and fitful. Neither of them slept soundly due to the storm and the adrenaline surging through them. Holt stretched. As much as he would love to curl up to Torrey and snuggle, even drift back off, his mind refused to embrace the idea. It was as though he had had more coffee, and now the need to be busy or doing something pricked his conscience. He knew this state very well. All through law school, he studied or exercised when these spurts hit him. Jogging came to mind as he ticked off what he could do without waking Torrey.

Holt made his way out of the bedroom, calculating what path his run would take, given their crazy directions getting here. He remembered the side streets they turned down and a few of the odd names he glimpsed driving down the dark roads. The more he mentally backtracked their route, the clearer his course came. Three blocks down, four to five over and back would bring him within radius of the townhouse. If he made the circuit five times, he might get a half mile in. Maybe he would add another block with each lap until he got in a mile.

Ten minutes passed while Holt pulled on his clothes and shoes. He scribbled a note to Torrey letting her know where he was and when to expect him back. Mischa and Doxie stirred as he laid the note on the nightstand Torrey used. His cell number stood out in large numbers at the bottom. He blew her a kiss and closed the bedroom door behind him.

Holt turned on his Bluetooth earpiece, synchronized it with his phone, and trotted toward the front door. He stopped. Hunger gnawed at him. His stomach growled. Holt moved to the refrigerator. Opening the freezer, he grabbed the first package of meat he came across. Two eight-ounce flank steaks grilled with vegetables sounded good. He tossed the steaks in the refrigerator. He'd marinate them when he returned.

Softly whistling an oldie-but-goodie he remembered, Holt stepped out the door, clicking the door quietly closed behind him. He fast stepped down the three front steps and broke into a brisk pace by the time he reached the sidewalk. He waved to several people as he turned the first corner. Sun greeted him as the clouds parted. Another runner caught up to him. It was Torrey's new neighbor from across the street. They nodded to each other as they fell in step together.

"Jon's dad, right?" Holt panted as he picked up his pace, matching the gent next to him.

"Yes. I'm Elbert. Most folks call me Bert." Bert smiled, keeping stride with Holt. "How far you want to go?"

"I usually do two miles. You know the neighborhood?" Bert's quick nod and point indicated straight ahead. Holt shrugged. "I'll follow you, but don't lose me."

Bert laughed. "I use to run track and long-distance events. I know how to pace myself to keep up with the pack."

Holt watched as Bert took off down the sidewalk. He hoped he was as nimble as Bert when he reached his golden years.

Halfway through their third lap of the ten-block radius, Holt's Bluetooth beeped. He nodded as Bert passed. Holt slowed down to answer the call. Bert stopped at the end of the street waiting for Holt to catch up.

"Holt Addison, how can I help you?" Holt resumed his pace closing the distance between he and Bert. Bert took off again as Holt got closer.

"Hey, big brother." Gwen's warm tone and teasing came across loud and clear. Holt smiled.

"What ya need, pest?" Gwen's snort and short laugh deepened Holt's growing smile.

"Wanted to make sure you're okay first."

"Yes. Got to shelter before the deluge opened up." Holt jogged in place next to Bert as they waited for cars to clear a main intersection.

"Good. I'll be quick, as I'm using my cell as a backup line for the shelter's phone until it's working again."

Holt nodded as he crossed the street, taking the lead on his and Bert's next lap.

Almost back to Torrey's, Gwen's voice took on a different, more serious tone. "You sent a woman and her two children to me last night."

"Is there a problem?" Holt glanced to Bert and held up his hand. "Gwen, give me a moment, please."

Holt covered the mike with his hand. "Thanks, Bert. This is my sister. I need to talk to her for a bit. I'll catch up with you if I'm able."

Bert held out his hand. "No problem. I always shake the hand of a good runner. You got form, boy. Next time you're over, look me up and we'll get a true two-mile run in."

Holt shook Bert's hand. "You bet. Thanks again."

Holt entered the back patio through the side gate he remembered. He didn't want to track any more dirt and mud into the living room than there already was, thanks to Mischa and Doxie.

"Gwen, I'm back. Tell me what's going on."

Holt drummed the table with his fingers as Gwen explained the woman's problem. Fifteen minutes later, Holt knew he needed to talk to his client. Tomorrow would be soon enough. No judge would act without evidence or cause.

"Tell Clarissa she has a lawyer. Don't worry about money. I've got her covered. Where are the kids?"

"I got them placed with family her ex doesn't know about. I hated splitting them up. To keep them safe and out of sight, I had to." Gwen sighed.

Holt knew that sigh. "Sis, let me handle this. Finding the guy and beating the shit out of him isn't going to solve the problem."

"I know. His kind doesn't learn until they are in jail or never learn 'cuz they're dead." Gwen finished bringing Holt up to date on what the shelter's general attorney had done.

"Gwen, I need to get a shower and check on Torrey. I got stranded at her place. I'll be in touch tomorrow. Love ya."

"Sure, Holt. Love you, too."

Holt opened the sliding glass doors and entered the kitchen. Torrey screamed as she came around the corner from the hall, a baseball bat in her hands.

"Whoa, sweetie," Holt yelled as he caught her forward swing, stopping the bat from connecting with his stomach.

"Where have you been? I woke up and you were gone. Now you come back sweaty and muddy." Torrey panted in between outbursts. She let go of the bat, backing off.

"Take a deep breath and sit down." Holt laid the bat on the counter and reached for the chair closest to him. "Didn't you get my note?"

"What note?" Torrey dropped into the chair and folded her arms tight around her.

Holt reached toward Torrey, his hand met air. Sounds of her chair scooting away followed.

"Okay," Holt started, grabbing the other nearby chair. He dropped into it. Leaning forward, he worked his hand into Torrey's. Christ, he'd never seen her this worked up. Bat aside, he was glad she kept something around to defend herself.

Touching her made sense. He inched his fingers along her palm until he found her wrist and felt her pounding pulse. She was very agitated. Even her breathing remained short and shallow. "I left you a note on your nightstand. I explained what I was doing and where I was going."

Torrey groaned more as he continued. "I even left my cell phone number so you could call if you needed me. Sweetie, I'm sorry I spooked you like that."

Torrey worried her lip with her teeth and inhaled. Letting go a deep sigh, she dropped one arm while raising her eyes to Holt's. "Waking up finding you gone without a word was one thing. But when I looked for you and didn't see you anywhere, I got worried."

"Worried?" Holt's tone rankled her. Her fear and worry, however valid in her mind and thoughts, apparently baffled him.

"Yes, *worried*. I didn't see your gym bag or got an answer when I called out your name." Torrey dabbed at her eyes with the sleeve of her robe.

"I put my bag in the front closet on my way out to jog. Leaving it lying around didn't make sense. Okay, so I pick up after myself."

Torrey felt her heart slow as she breathed deeper. "All right, I might have missed a thing or two. What note are you talking about?"

Holt rose tugging her hand with his. "Come on. The one I left in plain sight next to the clock."

Torrey stood, trying to work her hand free. "If it was in *plain sight*"—she liked how Holt winced at her emphasis on his words—"I would have seen it."

Holt moved behind her. His hand rubbed across her shoulder. "Let's go see what is on the nightstand, shall we?"

Torrey trotted down the hall; sure she was going to win the argument. As she entered the bedroom, Siam shot out from under the bed, followed by Mischa and Doxie.

"Did the motley crew wake you?" Holt's chuckle eased some of her apprehension.

"Yes, those three get rowdy at the damnedest times." Torrey spun around, facing Holt as she moved into the bedroom. "I don't see any note."

Holt stepped by her as he moved toward the bed. "I laid the note here." He sat as he pointed to the space next to the clock. "I wanted you to see it when you sat up or rolled over."

Torrey gasped as her gaze followed the direction Holt pointed. On the floor, wedged between the side of the nightstand and the wicker trashcan, lay a yellow piece of paper. She shot Holt a sheepish grin and bent to retrieve the paper. "Umm—I'm sorry," she offered, clutching the paper in her hand.

"I should swat you with your ass temptingly available to me. Instead, I'll accept the apology and offer to cook you dinner." Holt rose, cupped his hand, and patted her bottom.

Torrey smiled. "What you cooking, big guy?" She tilted her head, batted her eyes at him, and stuck out her tongue.

Holt laughed, closed the distance between them, and tugged her to him. "Keep it up and you might get more than you bargained for."

Torrey's laughter vibrated over him. Holt hugged her tighter to him. "On second thought, I need a shower and food before I attempt that feat. Steak and some vegetables sound appealing?"

"Sure. I'll defrost the steaks while you shower. Then grab one myself." Torrey wiggled, trying to free herself from him.

"Be still, woman, or you may find yourself appeasing my baser needs first." Holt crushed Torrey to him and released her. "Now go thaw the steaks lest I change my mind."

Torrey's mirth echoed as she trotted down the hall. Holt whistled as he stripped off his sweaty clothes and muddy shoes in the guest room. He needed a quick shower.

As hot water cascaded over him, he worked through the information Gwen had given him. Clarissa faced a huge problem if her ex decided to pursue his claim. Grand theft auto or kidnapping by themselves was bad enough. Together and a judge might move faster than Holt liked. He needed to find out where Clarissa's ex was. More details and a bit of research might buy them time. Holt hoped Torrey's internet access was up. He would research things after dinner and talking to Gwen.

Holt smiled as he pulled on the high-water jeans after examining the seams. A loose belt loop here and there explained the earlier thread pops he heard. He inhaled as he tugged his shirt over his head. "Something smells wonderful," he called out as he moved into the hall and made his way into the kitchen.

"I put some rolls on to bake. The steaks are defrosting in the microwave. I'm gonna shower." Torrey stood on her tiptoes and brushed her lips over his. "I'll see you in a few."

Holt watched as Torrey disappeared into her bathroom. There was an air of satisfaction and rightness to their brief exchange. Maybe, just maybe, his heart was leading him in the right direction.

Holt slid the steaks under the broiler as he heard the shower cut off. He noted the time. He hoped Torrey was hungry. He loved a good salad with his steak. The split potatoes he put into the oven after microwaving them would add to the carbs they would need if the rest of their night turned as frisky as their day.

Chapter Twenty

Torrey wiped her mouth, sighed, and raised her wine glass in salute. "Fine meal. My stomach and taste buds thank you."

Holt nodded. He reached for the last of the rolls. "I enjoy a woman who appreciates good food and the cookHe split the roll, offering her half.

"No, thanks. I want some of that marble fudge cake we whipped up before we sat down to eat. Timer shows ten minutes left." Torrey refilled her wineglass. "When did you learn to cook?"

Holt bit into his roll. He chewed, mulling over his answer. He washed the bread down with a swallow of wine. "I learned to cook back in college."

Torrey sat her glass down. She leaned forward. "How come you never offered to cook for me before?"

Holt arched his eyebrows and stared at her. "Where would I've found a kitchen to do so? Last we spoke, I was graduating and you were facing your senior year."

Torrey snorted, rolled her eyes toward the ceiling as if she actively pondered Holt's question. She glanced sideways at him, looked upward again, and bit her lip to keep from laughing. "Okay, so I asked a dumb question. Still, if you learned to cook in college, who taught you?"

Holt sat upright. "Grandma Getty. When Stuart and I started bringing friends home for break or the weekends, she made us pitch in and help. Said two young men might have to batch it for a while so we best learn how to fend for ourselves, because she wasn't moving in with us or us with her. A southern lady needed her rest not endless hours of unrest with two young men in the house, much less their horny libidos and girlfriends."

Torrey clapped her hand over her mouth. She struggled to keep from yelping as laughter threatened to overtake her. She inhaled sharply and tried to exhale through her nose. Instead, a huge snort sounded followed by squeaks of muffled laughs. Holt handed her a napkin. His smile grew the harder she tried to stifle her merriment.

Torrey wiped her eyes. "Oh, my goodness. I'm sorry. Having met Grandma more than once when Stuart had us over for the holidays, I can hear her saying that with her southern drawl and hands on her hips, looking at the two of you over her reading glasses."

Holt picked up his wine glass, swirled the contents, and drank. "My mother often said she didn't have to worry about Stuart and me getting into any trouble with Grandma looking after us. Poor Stuart knew that if he caught shit from his parents and Grandma found out, he was in over his head. It's a wonder he ever got laid 'cause I'm sure he heard Grandma every time he even looked at a girl with interest."

Torrey's open mouth made Holt smirk. "You didn't know?"

"Know what?"

"Grandma told Stuart the facts of life and handed him his first box of condoms. She asked him when we went home on our first break from college if he'd figured out how to use them yet and not as party balloons either. Seems she caught him in junior high making water balloons out of them." Holt stood, reached for Torrey's glass.

Torrey clapped both hands over her mouth. Slowly her hands slid down her front and crossed near her stomach. Holt glanced to her face. Was she all right?

Tears rolled down Torrey's cheeks, her smile growing by the minute. She began pounding the table as laughter escaped her tightened lips. "Oh, oh—poor Stuart," she managed to get out.

Holt nodded and carried their dishes to the sink. "I love that woman as if she were my own Grandma. Mother said her parents would have loved Grandma. Too bad they died before I was born. Dad's family split up so many times, I can't count how many steps and relatives I've got anymore."

Torrey followed with the rest of the dishes. "You asked about using my computer before we ate. What do you need?"

"Gwen called while I was jogging. Remember the woman and kids from last night?" Holt leaned against the counter as Torrey loaded the dishwasher.

"Yes, I meant to call her to check on them. I got—*uhmm*—distracted." Torrey winked at Holt. "Let's see if my internet is working."

Torrey led the way into the living room and to the corner area that housed her home office. She checked all the connections before sitting down. "Given the way the trio's been acting, I'm glad they stayed away from here. Siam heads for high ground when Mischa and Doxie start chasing him."

Holt smiled, shaking his head. "We'll have to see what we can do about getting things cleared out of the way once we can get out and about, okay?"

Torrey shrugged. "I'll turn on the news if the system boots up. I didn't see a paper earlier."

"When I was out I ran into Jon's dad, Bert. He led me on a ten-block loop. We passed two major intersections. Traffic was getting through even though the lights were out. I believe that was Magnolia and Bellhowell."

Torrey glanced over her shoulder as the computer chimed. "That is the main drag into our section. How many cars did you see?"

Two key strokes later and the local paper's website loaded. Photos from the bridge and flooded areas they'd encountered littered parts of the front page. Torrey scrolled down the page looking for updates on utilities and other areas. "Oh shit," she cursed, her finger tapping the screen.

Holt leaned closer, reading over her shoulder. "Sixty thousand without lights up and down the coast. Several hundred in Cascade Bay still without power. Damn, that's a lot."

"One hell of a storm," Torrey countered.

"One fucking hell of a derecho," Holt commented, pointing to the headline above her hand.

"Well, at least we can get out if necessary. I brought us in the back route as it is closer since we weren't too far from the store at that point." Torrey shoved back from her desk. "Go ahead and do what you need. The printer is in the cabinet next to the desk. Plenty of paper and ink."

Torrey walked past Holt as he sat down. "No more coffee for sure. How about some herbal tea and cake? The timer just went off." Two beeps sounded followed a series of louder ones.

"Sounds good. I left my cell phone in the guest room. Can you get it for me?" Holt signed into his e-mail account. "Gwen said she'd text me when she sent me her email."

After five phone calls, three bouts of cussing and muttering, and two long e-mails, Holt ran his hands through his hair. He glanced at the wall clock close to the desk. "Midnight? How did it get so late?" He rose, wiping his hands on his shirt.

Torrey smiled, laying the book she read beside her on the couch. "Somewhere between your second call to Gwen and your other numerous items, time went by. I asked you about things at the two-hour mark. You grunted and held up two fingers. About that time Gwen texted me, saying you were looking over the brief the shelter general attorney filed blocking extradition of the children until a judge ruled on the validity of Clarissa's ex's claim."

"Shit, Torrey, I get absorbed in my work. Especially when it's someone like Clarissa. I'm sorry I neglected you." Holt held out his hand.

"There's no neglect to apologize for. I saw a side of you I didn't know about. Gwen was right when she added in her final text to me you're the right man for the job. You dedicate yourself to those that need you and even more so to the ones you care about." Torrey placed her bookmark in the book and closed it. As she laid the book on the coffee table, her gaze met Holt's. "I'm finding this is one of the things I love about you."

Torrey stood, dusted her hands on her pants, and started to turn. Holt blocked her path. "One of the things you love about me? You love me?"

Torrey licked her lips, looked down, and counted to three before answering him. "I think so. At least, I'm pretty sure I do."

He cupped her chin, tilting her head back until he looked into her eyes. His eyes sparkled as his smile grew. His fingers tangled in her hair as his face came closer. "I like the sound of those words."

Holt's lips brushed hers. Bolts of static charges passed between them. It was as though the world and time stopped. Nothing mattered but the two of them. Torrey inhaled, snuggled deeper into Holt's embrace, and closed her eyes. Fear almost kept her from saying what her heart cried out. She'd worry about what next in a few moments. For now, nothing else mattered.

Chapter Twenty-One

Ten hours later

Torrey bolted upright in bed. Covers fell off her. Her hand lay where she'd placed it two minutes earlier, beside her in the cold spot that before Holt had occupied. Where was he?

As her vision cleared, the room came into focus. She immediately glanced at her nightstand. Her eyes searched the table. Nothing unusual there. Eight a.m. She'd slept sounder and deeper than she normally did. Even Mischa and Doxie were zonked out on the foot of the bed. Siam was curled up next to them.

Torrey blinked and looked back toward the mirror. Something caught her attention as she squinted. A small yellow item appeared stuck to her mirror. Tossing back the sheet and blanket, she scooted to the end of the bed and stood. She stepped over her slippers. Silence greeted her as she moved past the open door and the hall. She took a deep breath as she halted in front of the dresser. She could make out her name scrawled in Holt's handwriting.

Her hand shook as she reached for the paper. She hoped the inevitable hadn't happened. Last night more than once, Holt had jumped when his phone rang. His knack for deeply concentrating on his work intrigued her as well as reminded her of his prowess at figuring things out. He loved reading mysteries and working crossword puzzles, he admitted. In college, he read because he had to. Torrey smiled as images came back of Holt mugging as she scolded him about not keeping up with their English Literature class. Clenching the paper in her hand, Torrey backed up to the bed and sat down.

As she opened the taped-shut sides, Siam yawned, stretched, and curled up in her lap purring. Torrey petted him as she read Holt's note.

Torrey love,

You were deep asleep when I got the call. I didn't want to wake you.

What I feared happened. Clarissa's ex got a judge to start extradition proceedings. The police are picking her up between 8 and 10. I've got to get home, pack, and meet her at the shelter. Gwen called with the news. I don't know how long this is going to take. I'll be in touch ASAP.

I love you,

Holt

Torrey sighed as she read the note again. A lone tear threaten to work its way past her eye where it pooled. She patted Siam and wiped her face on her shoulder. As bare flesh rubbed her face, she smiled. Last night Holt had insisted on holding her nude and just breathing together as sleep claimed them. His last words warmed her as she remembered them. His deep tenor voice had sung two lines of their favorite slow dance song back in college before his first snore overtook him. The refrain of the Bee Gee's "To Love Somebody" echoed in her thoughts as Torrey pulled her robe on. With her slippers on, she padded down the hall, humming the tune.

She stopped humming as two more pieces of paper caught her eye. One was on the guestroom door and the other on the bathroom door. She snorted and grinned as another caught the corner of her eye on the bathroom mirror. Its folded corner stood out to ensure she saw it, she bet. Scanning all three, she laughed. Holt wanted to be sure she knew he left because he had to, not because he snuck out or had a change of heart. Bless him and who he'd become. Two years and never that far from each other once they'd returned to Cascade Bay, who knew they'd end up knowing they were right for the other without anyone setting them up. Well, almost without any help. Joanna figured she needed a lay. Stuart figured sex fixed a lot of things. They both knew Torrey didn't go for one-night stands or at least needed some connection with the person before she slept with them.

Torrey laughed hard as she made her way into the kitchen. Yellow Post-its stood out on half of her cabinets as well as several of them on the coffeemaker. She curled her toes deeper into her slippers as she read the one closest to her. In quick sketches, Holt illustrated a *love you* message. Torrey pulled each paper down, stacking them together. She hurriedly crossed the living room, placing them on her desk as she reached for her ringing cell phone. She'd forgotten it last night as Holt carried her to bed in his arms.

"Torrey here." Laughter answered. "Joanna?" Torrey held the phone away from her as the laughter grew in volume.

"Ye—ss. Stuart, stop. Stop tickling me." Joanna's muffled voice called out further for Stuart to halt and let her talk.

"Want me to call back in a few?" Torrey knew a few might be hours before they were not busy with sex. Those two could get very distracted when sex and nudity came together.

"No, I need to talk to you." Joanna's breathy sigh came through loud and clear.

"Problems?" Torrey padded back into the kitchen. She pulled a chair out and sat.

"Here, no. There, yes. Paula called. The store has water damage. She's there now. She couldn't reach you on the house phone. Can you check with her on what's going on?"

Torrey looked at the kitchen clock. With any luck, she could be there in forty-five minutes. She needed food, coffee, and a shower. Of course, as if on cue, Mischa and Doxie followed by Siam ran into the kitchen. They sniffed their food bowls and glared at her. "Um, I'll call her now. Probably be a bit before I can get down there. Just woke up, you know."

Joanna's muffled laughter started again. "Stuart, go back and finish drying off. I'll ask about Holt in a minute. You don't need to talk to him now. We've got more sightseeing to do once we get off the plane."

"Off the plane?" Torrey wondered how long Joanna and Stuart's vacation turned into an elopement and honeymoon was going to last.

"Oh, yes." Joanna's pitch picked up as she started explaining. "We're taking a four-day jaunt to the Grand Canyon. We won some crazy drawing the hotel is having. I'm gonna be out of phone range and contact. It appears we're going camping and horseback riding through the canyon. I'll tell you about it when we get back. Tell Holt Stuart says hi."

Before Torrey could say Holt wasn't around, Joanna ended the call. A sharp beep sounded. Torrey glanced down at her phone. The low battery icon flashed rapidly at her. "Shit," Torrey cursed, rummaging around her desk to find the charger. Three beeps later, her phone sat charging.

"Okay, you rascals," Torrey called out as she entered the kitchen. "Food time." Mischa and Doxie yipped as she poured dry food into their bowls. Siam sat on his lofty perch, atop the refrigerator, swishing his tail. Torrey picked up his bowl and set it on the counter. She knew better than to feed him next to the dogs. Animal food fights weren't pretty, and she needed to get herself fed if she was going to make it out on time. With the coffee brewing, Torrey trotted down the hall, wondering if Gwen had updates on Clarissa.

Torrey toweled her hair dry ten minutes later. She'd never showered this fast before. This was a new first for her. Maybe love continued to produce changes in folks. Good ones along with bad ones, from what she'd experienced. Another topic to discuss with Holt when they talked again. They had much to learn about each other still and yet knew a lot already.

As she pulled on her clothes, Torrey glanced toward the bed. Did the pillow still carry Holt's scent? Christ, she missed him horribly and it was only hours since they'd separated, according to the time he put on his notes. How bad did she have it? How far had she fallen? Two days and nights together with incredible sex and some sharing didn't mean they could last a lifetime, did it? Hell, Holt hadn't even mentioned beyond a few days out as they talked over the last two. Torrey caught her breath. Oh, man, was she in deep, and that meant he could hurt her again.

Torrey forced her focus on the good that had happened in the last two days. She recounted the times Holt had helped her or shown a different side of him. Ones that she'd never seen or known about previously. As she tied her shoes, Torrey stopped her meandering thoughts and decided. Neither of them promised the other anything beyond seeing where things led. Right now, she had a store to worry about after she let the dogs out and ate.

Back in the kitchen, she filled her commuter mug as she nibbled toast. She carried her mug with her as she paced back and forth between the living room and the pantry, checking her lunch tote for items to take with her. Halfway through her fourth sip, she grimaced. "Black? Yuck, I hate black coffee. I've got to focus. How could I forget the cream and sugar?"

Mischa and Doxie yipped as her cell chimed. Then the house phone rang three times and quit. Two hard knocks rattled the front door. Torrey grabbed her cell phone, answering it as she raced toward the door. "Hello?" Torrey unlocked the door after peering out the peephole. Two policemen stood outside.

Torrey gulped harder as a tear-filled voice answered her. "Paula here. I set off the alarm. I didn't mean to."

Torrey calmed her down after telling her to wait at the store for her. "I'll be there shortly. Let me handle the police."

Ten tense minutes went by until Torrey pulled out of her garage. She would have been on her way sooner except her car threatened to not start. All she needed was more bad news. "Come on, car," Torrey pleaded, patting the steering wheel. "You can hold out a few more months. Please?"

Torrey rolled her eyes heavenward, mouthed a couple of prayers, and looked in her rearview mirror. If her flock of guardian angels were riding along, they knew how important it was to keep her wheels running until she figured out her finances. Slow summer sales and now water damage might mean a new car was further off than she liked.

Taking the long way around town with roads still under water or downed power lines along with a long line at the gas station put Torrey behind what she even told the police. After reassuring them Paula worked for her and that the alarm company only had her home phone number, Torrey agreed to meet them at the store. As she pulled in, two cop cars sat next to the front door with Paula outside talking to them. Two parking spaces over, a van from the local alarm company sat with its motor running. The man inside appeared to be having a rather animated conversation with someone on his cell phone. Torrey drummed her fingers on her steering wheel, inhaled twice, and let go a long sigh. It was going to be a long day. She just knew it.

As she locked her car door, she caught bits and pieces of Paula's explanation to the officers questioning her. "Yes, I know the code and I followed instructions to turn the damn thing off. How was I supposed to know water had shorted out the relays on the phone lines?"

Torrey rolled her eyes again and mouthed a few pleas for help. Boy, were her guardian angels getting their workout today. Paula's tear-filled voice wasn't helping the demeanor of the cops either. One had his hand on his hip. The other scribbled in his notebook. Torrey gulped the last of her cold coffee and straightened her posture. Time to assume her business-owner persona.

"Good morning, officers. Sorry I'm late. Detours and gas lines, you know." She hoped her smile reached her eyes because she needed good luck, given the looks on their faces as they left her place. She hoped the alarm guy could turn the silent alarm off.

"Ma'am, if you can get your alarm turned off, we'll be fine with writing this off as storm related. If you can't, well, then we have to figure out how to file the report." The police officer closest to Torrey nodded and continued scribbling in his notebook.

"My company says all I got to do is snip the wires coming out of the box if the electricity is off." The alarm guy shrugged as both police gave him an arched eyebrow response. "Look, I'm out of my league with this. I install them and disarm them if the electricity is off. If it's on, that is someone else. Techs have their specialty."

Paula moved away from the officers and motioned Torrey to her. "I came in the front because the back door had water running under it. I went through to the office, and the back wall is soaked. The window got blown out along with some stock covered with glass as well as water."

Torrey gripped her keys harder. How soon would the insurance company settle? Could a claims adjuster come out today? She doubted it. As soon as she got a handle on the alarm issue, Torrey knew what her next job was.

"Let's take this one thing at a time, Paula." Torrey touched Paula's arm. "You did the right thing. I'm sure the officers know that. Let me handle this. You go inside and find a pad where we can start writing down what needs fixing and inventory the stock as well."

Paula nodded and scooted inside. Torrey spent the next moments reassuring the officers that once everything was handled, she would file her statement. She watched the officers drive off. She hid her smile until they were well on their way. A few gift cards for their wives had them understanding that simplicity made sense. Knowing the chief of police personally also eased matters. Calling him later would help with getting her report filed and the issue eased into storm-related damage rather than an alarm call.

As Torrey entered the store, she heard the security tech and Paula yelling.

"I told you not to touch anything. I've got to figure out what wires go to what." Torrey picked up her pace as Paula answered.

"You said turn off the electricity. So I did. You should have turned on your flashlight first."

Torrey smiled as the tech cursed in a foreign language. Paula answered him right back. The silence following told her the man knew better than to treat Paula as stupid.

"Excuse me," Torrey said. She knocked on the open door. "Before either of you starts a war over who is to do what. How about this, Paula you write down what you know about the damage you found and I'll finish up in here."

Paula's breathy thank-you as she breezed past got to Torrey. Laughter followed as the tech kept cursing and examining wires.

Chapter Twenty-Two

Holt glanced at his watch. Four hours and three airports. If he had to fight another list of stand-by passengers... He drummed his fingers against his leg. He knew Clarissa was safe and had a public defender assisting her until he arrived. Thank goodness, the lawyer was an old classmate. The attorney-client privilege would allow more discussion once he took over. Until then, knowing bits and pieces only added to his angst. The other issue was Torrey.

No answer to any of his calls. Not even a reply to a quick e-mail he managed to get off before he left for the airport midafternoon. Was she okay? Had her cell phone died? He smirked, remembering leaving it on her desk in their haste to cuddle and sleep. Neither Joanna nor Stuart answered theirs either. He would have to wait until evening to try again. The attendant called his name, clearing him to board. Who knew traveling two states away could be such an undertaking?

Ketchum, ID

Holt yawned. An hour time difference and lack of sleep finally caught up with him. He wanted to hear Torrey's voice, say good night, and whisper "I love you" as they talked until both of them drifted off. One in the morning wasn't time to do that. He knew she had called Gwen, even though they hadn't talked. Gwen said she had a voice mail from her. Text messages didn't replace hearing the voice of the person he cared about. He missed Torrey. After two nights of having her close by, the bed felt coldly empty.

The puddle jumper plane from Boise delayed its departure due to the same storm that had stranded him with Torrey. Another four hours spent debriefing Clarissa and the public defender left Holt more tired than if he'd flown straight through. Damn Clarissa's ex for being part of the good-old-boy network. The judge's old-fashioned values hadn't helped either. Still, the marshal accompanying Clarissa made sure she was taken care of and settled in a decent hotel rather than jail. In the morning, Holt knew Clarissa would have to explain why she wasn't in a holding cell. Taking time to file the restraining order in Boise also bought them flexibility.

Holt scoffed as he flipped again through the repair estimate his assistant prepped for him on the car in question. Grand theft auto charges couldn't stick based on dollar value or if the car registration showed both Clarissa's and her ex's names. Holt suspected the ex was a control freak. He would soon find out how much control freaks didn't rule. Holt shook his head as he remembered Gwen's parting words. Punching the freak out in a dark alley wouldn't provide Holt as much pleasure as seeing him put away for battery and assault.

Laying the papers on his briefcase, Holt climbed into bed. He checked his cell to make sure it charged. He sent one last text, hoping to reach Torrey, letting her know she wasn't far from his thoughts and he would call her in the morning.

Cascade Bay

Torrey rolled over, plumping her pillow for the second time. Eight hours on her feet and her head spun with the numbers and figures that she needed to file the insurance claim. The claims adjuster had dropped by and done a preliminary assessment. If everything tallied what he said, shit was polite cussing. Her car would have to last much longer than what the mechanic said it would.

"God, I wish Holt were here." Torrey turned over again. She petted Siam who lay next to her, purring. Even his purrs weren't helping sleep find her. A loud beep sounded next to her. Torrey rolled on her back and picked up her cell phone off the nightstand. She smiled as she read Holt's text. She glanced at time stamp. She took a deep breath and didn't hesitate to respond. Within moments, Holt answered. After five minutes of texting back and forth, her phone rang.

"Hi, sexy," Holt's voice whispered. Torrey giggled. She couldn't help herself. She felt like a teenager again, sneaking in a late-night call with her boyfriend.

"Hi yourself," she replied. "Tell me about your day."

Holt's short laugh warmed her even more. Torrey touched her lips and traced her smile with her fingers.

"I'll keep it short. Too many details and we'll both be wide-awake when we need to sleep. Clarissa is down the hall from me at the same hotel. I'm not sure how the airlines deal with stand-by as much as they do. I booked my flight back as soon as I landed."

"What if you need to exchange your ticket?" Torrey wanted Holt back as quickly as possible. Waiting and patience were items she needed ample supply of right now.

"With ticket in hand, a hell of a lot easier than if I didn't." Holt's forced laugh told Torrey how tired and frustrated he was.

"I've heard that laugh before. Do I need to send bail money?" Torrey snickered, awaiting Holt's response. Instead, he yawned and remained quiet.

Torrey toyed with the edge of the sheet before she spoke. "Are you falling asleep on me?"

Holt yawned again. "Sorry, love. Yes. I need to be up in six hours. Ready to face a good old southern redneck from what I've learned as well as a stick-in-the-mud judge along with said redneck's lawyer. I best get some sleep."

Torrey smiled as Holt whispered what he would prefer to be doing before he ended the call. His soft "I love you" warmed away any lingering doubts she had for the moment. She was sure others would crop up and they would need tending. Until they did, Torrey didn't care. Sleep mattered more.

Siam rose, stretched, and curled up near her head, purring loudly. His blue eyes blinked twice before he fell asleep watching his mistress breathe deeply as sleep claimed her as well.

Two mornings later, Torrey dialed Holt's number. He'd left brief e-mails and texts while he and Clarissa sat through opening statements. His assistant took two statements from Gwen as to her actions concerning placement of the children and the center's child advocate's findings upon examination of the children both mentally and physically. Torrey wondered when her involvement would come into question. Holt reassured her that her name wasn't amongst the list the other side wanted to hear from.

On the third ring, Holt answered. "Hi there, sexy."

Torrey smiled more at the lilting pitch and upbeat tone of Holt's voice. "Sounds like things are going well."

Holt chuckled. "As well as can be expected. Anderson, Clarissa's ex, didn't think I would know about used cars and their worth. Thanks to Stuart's cousin Terrence, I blew their cover. The car isn't worth more than one thousand dollars if repairs are made, and the repairs cost more than the car is worth."

Torrey gulped air. She whistled through her teeth. "Meaning that car shouldn't have been on the road?"

"Bingo," Holt replied. "The car needed new tires as well as brakes. Anderson's little ploy didn't work. As to the theft, well, you can't steal what belongs to you. Seems he never took Clarissa's name off the title."

"Sounds like you got match and set handled. Congrats," Torrey offered. Silence greeted her. She waited as muffled noise sounded on the other end.

"Sorry, love, I've got to go. Judge wants to know more about the children. I've got to deal with his need-to-know statements. I'll try to call later." Holt ended the call before Torrey could say "I love you." Not that it mattered. They signed their e-mails "love you." Doubts crept up when she paused in her day. Could they keep going when Holt returned?

Torrey leaned on the counter, surveying the amount of traffic whizzing up and down the street in front of the shop. As things returned to normal, business began to trickle in. The claims adjuster's latest voice mail stated the amount Torrey would receive was twice what she estimated once all supporting documents were in. Luck seemed to be going her way. Why couldn't she get rid of the apprehensions nagging her about her and Holt?

Paula waved as she exited her car. Torrey raised her hand to wave back. Her mouth dropped open. The alarm company van pulled in next to Paula. The same tech got out, leaned over, and kissed Paula on the lips. Torrey didn't need to be closer to know Paula blushed. The smile on her face spoke volumes. Matchmaking happened when one least expected it. How many other couples came together knowing less about each other than she and Holt did?

Torrey mulled over her thoughts as Paula and the tech chatted briefly. He hugged Paula twice and left. As Paula entered the store, Torrey knew one thing for sure. No matter what happened going forward, she wanted to try to build upon what she and Holt had started. Was their foundation solid enough to do so? She was almost sure it was.

Holt held Clarissa's hand as the judge entered the courtroom. Holt knew waiving a jury trial made sense. Jury selection and testimony along with the additional expenses of bringing all their supporting witnesses to Ketchum would have dragged things out and hindered both sides more than presenting their evidence in the closed hearing. As Clarissa rose, she visibly shook. Holt clasped her hand tighter. Her eyes met his. He nodded. He felt certain they would win. Anderson had flubbed up more than once during cross-examination. The judge even eyed him with a stare that said *I don't believe you.*

"Be seated." The judge banged his gavel. "First I'm going to say my piece. Then I'll hear any last-minute remarks from the lawyers. No outbursts from either party."

Holt snuck a quick sideways glance at Anderson. His mouth opened twice. His lawyer nudged Anderson hard in the ribs with his elbow both times. Holt was sure he knew how fed up Anderson's lawyer was. The man couldn't keep his mouth shut for long. Only a contempt of court warning got him to quit talking when he took the stand, and his lawyer had rested their case.

Holt bit his lip to keep from smirking as the judge glared at Anderson. Holt squeezed Clarissa's hand and glanced at her. Her lips moved as though she prayed. She had more than once mentioned her faith and absolute trust in God to keep her safe. Holt hoped her prayers were heard and answered.

"Now," the judge began in an authoritative voice. He straightened the papers he'd leafed through. "I don't know where you two lost sight of your reasons for getting married. It's not my job to decide that. I know from your testimony and the evidence presented that neither of you is good for the other any longer. I'm not a divorce judge. However a friend of mine is and your divorce decree and papers are here for both of you to sign."

The silence grew and lingered as the judge pulled two papers from the stack in front of him. "According to two reliable body shops, the vehicle in question is not worth repairing. And the insurance adjuster confirms their reports. As the car is registered in names of the defendant and the plaintiff, no theft has occurred. However, since the defendant needs transportation, I'm fining the plaintiff the cost of repairs based on the estimates for his contempt restitution unless he prefers to serve time and have his pay garnished. And the vehicle will be titled in her name only and registered as hers. Bill of sale to read one dollar. Said moneys for repairs and miscellaneous fees will be paid to the court and sent to the defendant via her attorney."

The judge signed the papers and handed them to the bailiff. "Next are the kidnapping charges. Based upon the evidence and the sworn affidavits along with the defendant's testimony, *and...*"

Holt even shivered at the judge's emphasis and his cold gaze at Clarissa and Anderson. "It takes two parents to raise children. You, sir," the judge continued, pointing his gavel at Anderson, "are a disgrace to fatherhood. You don't know your children's ages or anything much about them. Custody awarded to the mother pending divorce settlement along with restraining order granted. Their whereabouts as well as your ex's will not be known or revealed to you. And you are signing the divorce papers before you leave these chambers. Case closed." The judge scribbled his name on the last set of papers in front of him and handed them to the bailiff.

Holt helped Clarissa stand as the judge stepped down. He lingered near the door to his chambers. He kept watching Anderson and the bailiff as Anderson scrawled his name across several forms. His attorney signed as well. The bailiff witnessed the signatures. He stopped by Holt. "Your client signed and filed her papers months ago. His Honor will make sure these are filed and handled by the domestic courts. You'll receive a copy within a few weeks."

Holt thanked him and nodded to the judge as he took the papers from the bailiff. The door to the judge's chambers thudded closed.

Anderson headed out first, his lawyer close behind. He didn't even look back. His shoulders slumped as he scuffed his way out the door. Holt didn't like to see anyone that beat up, even by the law. People like Anderson got what they deserved. How much time he would get for the assault and battery charges the judge ruled on earlier in the week remained to be decided.

"Come on, Clarissa. We've got a plane to catch. We can handle the rest of this from home." Clarissa's weak smile and nod punched Holt in the gut. It would take her awhile to understand she was free. If she took Gwen up on her offer, she would be safe and free with a job awaiting her.

Holt blinked back tears as Clarissa hugged him, smiling and crying herself. She tried to wipe her eyes with the tissue she'd crumpled in her fisted hands awaiting the judge's decision. The two-hour wait broke more than her resolve. She'd confided she wanted nothing more than a fresh start and peace along with a healing that allowed her to trust herself as well as others once again. Holt silently vowed he would help as much as possible. He knew Torrey would, too, as soon as they got a chance to talk and reunite.

Holt stepped away after hugging Clarissa tightly to him one more time. She shook and shivered some before returning his embrace. Her nod as he questioned if she was okay told him she worked through her first response to pull away. It would take time and a gentle understanding. He hoped she found someone she could build a future with. She and her kids deserved the best.

As Holt gathered his documents and placed them in his briefcase, the bailiff called his name, motioning him toward the judge's chambers.

"His Honor wanted you to have these copies. The official decree and lump sum support settlement will follow in a week. His Honor has friends in high places. They knew about the situation. Anderson is going away for a while. Safe trip home, sir."

Holt thanked the bailiff. Clarissa sat openmouthed at the table. It appeared her luck was already turning around.

Chapter Twenty-Three

Three weeks later

Holt looked around McClark's. Where had the time gone? Stuart and Joanna were due back tonight. Stuart had asked him to meet for a drink and snacks after work. His stress on the word *talk* had Holt wondering what was up. Every time the door opened and the attached bell chimed, Holt checked to see if Stuart entered.

Sipping his beer, Holt leaned back against the booth. He wondered if Torrey was home from her buying trip and funding seminar she attended. Her short calls and brief e-mails helped some. Having her home and close-by to strengthen their growing connection and budding relationship made sense. How soon they'd be able to focus on that was another thing.

Holt reached for his cell phone. It lay on the table next to his beer. The phone began vibrating and moving across the table. The caller ID read *Torrey*. His smile grew as he touched the answer button.

"Hey there." His smile grew as Torrey answered.

"Hi, handsome. I'm at the airport waiting for my flight to board." Her tired voice wrapped around him as if she were next to him.

"You mean you're actually coming home?" Holt chortled at Torrey's reply.

"You bet. I'm tired and ready to stay put. God, I hope Joanna and Stuart get back soon. I need a vacation." Torrey's breathy laughter increased the warmth exploding in Holt's groin.

"What did you learn?" He scooted forward on the booth seat, hoping to adjust his nether region without having to reach down and tug his zipper away from his hard-on.

"We've got a good chance at growing Ladies' Satisfaction into a franchise within two states. The foundation has a reputation that reaches farther than anything Joanna and I knew about. Seems Gwen and Clarissa are good public relations reps." Torrey's sigh and muffled yawn indicated how tired she was.

"Sounds like you gained a lot of good information and also know where to grow the business next. Let me know how I can help." Holt waited, knowing he'd dropped a lure. He wanted Torrey to snag it. Reeling her in and entwining them more would be lovely. How deep was she ready to go?

"I may take you up on that offer. We need to work on splitting the foundation and the store into two separate entities. I met with our accountant before I left, and we need our charitable status official with the IRS."

"Got ya. We'll talk about it over dinner, say, tomorrow night?" Holt crossed his fingers. He wasn't superstitious, but an added enhancement never hurt.

Torrey's mirth made him want to pump his fist in the air and mouth a silent *yes*. "How about dinner and overnight, studly?"

Holt dropped his hand to his leg and leaned forward. He looked sideways. No one appeared to be watching. He slid his hand down his thigh until his hand rested between his legs. He grabbed the inner seam of one jean leg and then the other, pulling and tugging. Much more talk like this and he would need ice to cool down his obviously hard cock.

"Do you need a ride home from the airport?" Holt deliberately changed the subject. He put his hand back on the table, picked up his beer, and swallowed part of it.

Holt scribbled down Torrey's arrival time and airline as she talked. "If Joanna doesn't pick me up, I'll take you up on that ride. Otherwise, tomorrow night is good. We'll talk more in the morning. Love you."

Before he could respond, Torrey ended the call. Holt had caught part of the announcement in the background. Her flight was preparing to board. In a few hours, Torrey might be in his arms and he in her bed. Holt smirked as his conscience corrected his grammar and sequence of events...in Torrey's arms and then her bed. His grin widened as possibilities came to mind.

"Gee, you never grin like that with me." Stuart's voice knifed through Holt's growing fantasy like ice chilling a hot drink.

Holt looked up. Stuart stood next to the table, grinning worse than *Alice in Wonderland*'s Cheshire cat. Giving Stuart an arched eyebrow and stare over his glasses, Holt shrugged. "About time you got here."

Stuart laughed as he slid into the booth opposite Holt. "Sorry. Joanna and I had a family meeting we *had to* attend. Besides, we got back a couple of days ago."

Holt couldn't help but notice Stuart's emphasis on *had to*. "I'll buy you a beer and some hot wings. I'm still working on mine. You got back early." Holt motioned to a server close to them.

As soon as the wings and beer were served, Stuart leaned forward. "Thanks for the beer. I need this bad. Yes, and we're glad we did." He downed a third before setting the glass down.

Holt picked up a wing, bit into it, and chewed. He wiped his mouth before speaking. "Give me the lowdown on this family meeting."

Stuart nodded as he nibbled a wing. "Two words. *Grandma Getty.*"

Holt covered his mouth quickly. He grabbed two napkins from the dispenser on the table. His eyes watered as he tried to keep from snorting beer up his nose and not bust out laughing. Lord, what was that old woman up to now? Holt motioned for Stuart to continue.

"Grandma is on the warpath." Stuart finished his wing and bit into another.

"Warpath? Grandma? What set her off?" Holt decided against risking another mouthful of anything until Stuart replied.

"Wedding. No family present and no minister. Rather one of her choosing." Stuart tossed bones on to the plate next to him. He sipped at his beer, leaned back, and glared at Holt.

"Dude, why you glaring at me? I had nothing to do with setting off Grandma." Holt sat sideways in the booth, angling his arm across the back of his seat. The booth behind them was empty.

Stuart sighed. "You always joked about how eloping made more sense than dealing with family issues and who to invite and why. Remember we discussed this more than once during college."

"And you're telling me because of this you asked Joanna to marry you on your vacation?" Holt shook his head.

"Well, yeah, and Joanna saying she thought Vegas was a perfect honeymoon option besides saying yes. Got me a lecture on my impulsive nature for forty minutes from Grandma. Joanna said she smiled and was so nice her face hurts. And her karma quotient is overflowing with bonus points."

Holt snorted, set his beer down, and burst out laughing. "Sorry bro. This one you got into all on your own. Grandma isn't after me."

Stuart leaned forward on the table. "Guess again. You're on top of her list."

"*What?*" Holt struggled to keep his hand on the table and not shoot Stuart his middle finger along with the words.

"Between Grandma, my mother, and Joanna's, they've come up with a list of potential attendants and guest list. Your name and best man are number one on all of them." Stuart sat back and crossed his arms loosely against him. "Now try to get out of that one. Grandma even mentioned Torrey was the best one to pair you up with since they have her down as Joanna's maid of honor."

Holt swallowed hard. He pointed to himself. "Shit, how much have you said? Torrey's gonna have my ass over this."

Stuart laughed and smiled. "Ain't talked out of school, chum. And nothing other than Joanna mentioning you and Torrey were talking to each other again. Grandma nodded and said good. Her other words were 'about time those two got back together.'"

Holt coughed, gulped his beer, and vigorously shook his head. "Please, no matchmaking, Stuart. Call Grandma off. None of her voodoo dolls and love potions or charms either."

Holt bit his lip as two cold shivers warped over his neck and shoulders before icing down his spine. A chorus of *yeses* seemed to ring in his ears and echoed through his psyche. Holt snuck a sideways peek before clearing his throat. No one was close by or caught more than his quick reaction to Stuart's answer.

"No, nothing like that. Joanna and I agreed for the sake of the families and our future to a church wedding in two weeks. Grandma's church and her favorite deacon officiating. Say you'll be there, bro. I want ya there." Stuart laid his open hand palm up on the table.

Holt inhaled, counted in fives to a hundred, and considered his options. Stuart was the brother he never had. Three sisters between his mom and dad before they divorced and no children of their own other than stepkids since remarrying pushed hard on Holt's conscience. He would want Stuart at his wedding up there as best man, too. Another blast of cool air inched its way down Holt's neck. Holt rolled his eyes toward the ceiling. He blinked and blinked again. Two gray spots glowed and then vanished as *do what is right* rang in his ears. He knew better than to argue with spirits or give them too much due. Torrey and her guardian angels came up from time to time in their talks. Holt finished his beer. He set the glass down, leaned forward, and grasped Stuart's hand.

"I'm with you. Let me know where and when the tux fittings are. And I hope you didn't choose ridiculous colors."

Stuart's smile and sigh of relief cooled the apprehension building in Holt's gut. "You bet I will. And colors...Joanna is in charge of hers. Said simple black tuxes would be fine."

"How about another round of wings and drinks in celebration?" Holt raised his glass as their server passed by.

"Nothing alcoholic this time. I got a bride waiting for me at home, and I'm driving." Stuart gave his glass to the server.

Torrey tossed her carry-on bag in the backseat of Joanna's car. "Thanks for picking me up. Wasn't sure if you'd be back in time."

Joanna looked in the rearview mirror before pulling into oncoming traffic. She nodded as Torrey fastened her seatbelt. "When I got your voice mail about the damage and also needing to attend the seminar, I told Stuart we had to get back. He agreed, and we came in a few days ago."

"I appreciate you cutting things short. Have you eaten? I'm famished. The last session ran late." As if on cue, her stomach growled loudly, protesting its emptiness.

"There's a diner twenty minutes down the road. I've waited to eat with you." Joanna kept her eyes on the road.

Torrey noticed how flat Joanna's tone was. "You okay? Something bothering you?"

Joanna looked at Torrey as she stopped for a red light. "Bothering me as in bad? Yes and no. I'm that obvious?"

"We've been friends too long for me not to notice. But obvious, damn straight, girlfriend. Your tone is very flat." Torrey reached out and touched Joanna's arm. "Marriage troubles already?"

Joanna snorted as she changed lanes. "No marriage problems. Family issues, oh yeah."

Torrey winced at Joanna's emphasis on her last words. "I'm all ears, sister. Spill it."

Joanna pulled into the diner's parking lot. "Wait until we're inside, and bring my portfolio with you, please. I've got something in the trunk I need to bring in, too."

As their waitress left with their order, Joanna pulled a cloth swatch out of her tote bag. "What do you think of this color? Or this?" She placed another beside the first.

Torrey pulled the swatches to her. Mauve looked good on her with her fair complexion and hair color. The deeper ruby red also shimmered, reminding her of wine. Either color complemented her. "I like both colors. Either one would be nice alone. What are you considering them for?"

Joanna sat back, folded her hands, and spoke. "Grandma Getty."

Torrey sucked in air. "What? I don't get it." Had the woman taken up her magic again and wanted help making her dolls?

Joanna snickered. "Take that look off your face. Grandma is a good church-abiding woman. She's insisting Stuart and I have a church wedding with family and friends in attendance. Seems Vegas marriages aren't sacred enough in her mind."

Torrey sipped her water. She reached for a piece of bread and glanced at the colors again. "These are your color choices?"

"Remember Mary the seamstress who owns the bridal store two blocks over?"

"Yes, she sends a lot of business our way." Torrey buttered her bread and bit into it.

"These are the two colors she has ready-made dresses in. I wanted something my attendants can wear again. Since you're my maid of honor, you get to help me choose what color."

Torrey nodded as she chewed. She pointed to the ruby red color as she swallowed. "This is nice for a basic color. The mauve would accent nicely in flowers or shawls. Are you figuring sleeveless or strapless? And yes, I'm your maid of honor. We decided that back in high school. You ain't catching me off guard on that."

Joanna smiled. "I didn't think I would. Street-length dresses with cap sleeves and contrasting shawls sounds good. I've got a week from today to get you in and fitted. My other attendants are Stuart's cousin Abegail, or Abebi as we know her, along with a couple of other girls I know from college."

Torrey cut into her Chicken Coterie. "This smells wonderful. I'm on board. What about the others? Stuart's groomsmen?"

Joanna finished her sandwich. "Four as well for Stuart. Grandma insisted on pairing you up with Holt." Joanna paused as if waiting for Torrey to insist otherwise.

"Go on?" Torrey motioned with her knife and fork as she continued cutting and eating.

"Two of Stuart's college friends, Graham and Mitch, along with a cousin that is in town. Short notice but Grandma already has thirty-five RSVPs from the list of one-hundred and fifty she, Stuart's mom, and mine came up with."

"Swell. Nothing intimate about this gathering, eh?" Torrey pushed her plate away from her.

Joanna opened her portfolio. She flipped open the calendar. "I told Grandma and her crew that I wanted a catered reception with wine and beer along with two entrees and a simple cake. Grandma's eyes glowed when I said simple." Joanna ran her finger down the list next to the calendar page.

Torrey leaned closer. Reading upside down wasn't easy, but she made out several of the words. "We're good on help as repairs are done on the back wall. Paula welcomed the full-time hours, and the two part-timers will pick up the slack. Where do you need my help?"

An hour later, Joanna dropped Torrey at her place. Torrey waved as she drove off. The next two weeks were going to fly by. Most of the time Holt would be around and with her. Reconnecting would be easier and faster, given that.

Chapter Twenty-Four

Three days later

Torrey leaned back in her patio chair. Late summer evenings allowed Holt to fire up his grill and show her what he had learned from a chef whose case he'd taken. Foil packets lined the wire grate with Swai enclosed sprinkled with southwestern seasoning and a pat of unsalted butter. Next to the charcoal coals, ears of sweet white corn roasted.

She picked up her wine glass and sipped the dark burgundy-red contents. Tart cherry mixed with pears and purple grapes flavors flowed over her tongue. Holt's selection in the wine hadn't been wrong. The fish he'd grilled to perfection, moist and flakey, and the ears of corn complemented each other. Her salad of baby greens with goat and feta cheeses added the right amount of tang. Holt's suggestion of adding black olives with the Russian salad dressing to the greens balanced out the meal.

"I don't have a cat, so I can't say the feline has your tongue." Holt grinned, saluted her with his wine glass. "Why are you quiet?"

Torrey smiled, shaking her head. " A lot has happened. In many ways, it's like we picked up where we left off, and yet there's more."

Holt swallowed some of his wine, sat the glass down on the patio table. He cupped his chin with his hand as he leaned on his elbow. "I'm not sure what you're trying to say. I know I felt like I've known you for a long time. But there are times when I'm going 'huh' as I spend more time with you."

Torrey pointed at Holt. "Bingo! That's part of what I'm feeling, too."

Holt rose, and began gathering their dinner dishes. "How or why comes to mind as the next question."

Torrey picked up both glasses and their utensils before following Holt inside. "You wash, I'll dry," she offered, setting everything in the sink. "There's no sense in using the dishwasher."

Holt chuckled. "I like how well we work together. It's this that has me thinking we're gonna be good for the long haul."

Torrey swallowed, worried her bottom lip as she turned away from Holt and reached for the dishtowel. She'd been busy with other worries and issues the last two weeks. A huge feeling of doom showered over her. She shook and closed her eyes, wishing the impending sense of disaster would go away. The more she wished, the deeper the sensation went. She counted each breath she took, wondering what brought this on.

Holt glanced over his shoulder as he filled the sink with dishes and detergent. Torrey appeared preoccupied with something. As he turned off the hot water, he saw her shaking hands as she grasped the towel. He rinsed his hands and moved toward her.

"Honey, what's wrong?" Torrey faced him, tears running down her cheeks. Her weak smile grabbed him and clenched tighter around his heart. "Oh, babe, I'm sorry."

He closed the space between them, enfolded her in his arms, and cradled her close to him. "I don't know what brought this on. When you're ready, please tell me. I'm here for you."

Holt backed them across his kitchen until he stumbled against a chair. Kicking the chair out from under the table, he sat, taking Torrey with him so she sat on his lap. He kept her close, listening to her intermittent sobs and sniffles. He worked the towel out of her hands and dabbed at the remaining wet spots on her face as he leaned her back. He brushed his lips over hers and hugged her again. "When you're ready, I'm listening."

Torrey nodded, inhaling rapidly. She held her breath briefly. Unanswered questions, fears, and dread mixed with elation mixed in her mind. Joyous elation at Holt wanting to go for the long haul, and yet the obvious unknowns that neither of them had broached. What mattered more? Which came first? Torrey took a deep breath and let the prominent echo voice its concern.

"Why did you hurt me?" Torrey stood as she spoke. She pulled the towel from Holt's hands and wiped the rest of her face. She willed her heart to stop its fast pitter-patter and to slow with each breath she took. No good, the longer he remained quiet, looking at her with his mouth open, the harder and faster her heart beat. Unable to stand his anxious look as he closed his mouth, Torrey turned away and fumbled with pulling the other chair out. As she sat, she saw Holt's movements.

Holt stood and began pacing. Torrey's question caught him off-guard he wanted to yell and cuss. He knew this wouldn't solve the issue. Problem was he couldn't remember hurting her. Not since their reconnection and certainly not within the weeks they were apart, each of them had neither the time nor the energy to do more than keep up with business and their short nightly chats. The last two days passed without an incident that he could remember.

"I–I'm unsure how to respond." Holt stopped as he neared Torrey. "When did I do this?"

He watched Torrey place the wadded up towel on the table. She scooted to the edge of her chair, her hands palms down on her knees. Her feet flexed each time she breathed. Holt wanted to say stop. He'd seen such nervous fidgeting during court cases. He decided to leave well enough alone and let her be.

Torrey exhaled and spoke, her voice trembling. "When you started seeing Nancy. You never said what was going on. Not one bit of explanation. I had so many questions and needed so many answers."

Holt dropped into his chair. His mind raced with answers and questions of his own. None made sense in light of Torrey's revelation. Was there a sane answer he could give? He wasn't sure. "The old me was a dumb ass. I never saw the signs nor picked up on the signals. I—"

Torrey held up her hand. She cleared her throat before speaking. "I wish you wouldn't deprecate yourself. I'm probably to blame, too."

Holt's quick nod sent a short burst of calm cascading over her. He continued. His subdued tone got her attention. "Nancy and I lasted no more than three weeks. Weeks that I wished repeatedly were spent with you. By the time I broke things off with Nancy, you were gone. No one would tell me where you moved. I knew you stayed on campus, but I couldn't find out which dorm. Graduation was a few days off when I learned you had moved out and told no one your new address."

"I cowered and hid. Why did you wish the weeks were with me instead of Nancy?" Torrey held her breath. Holt's reply could make or break their future. Still part of her wanted to forgive the past and build upon the foundation they had now.

Holt's brief gaze and wink set off new ripples. Ripples that washed over her stomach and threatened to breach her floodwalls. Hastily built, floodwalls. Torrey motioned for Holt to go on.

"You said we'd gotten to be more than friends. Even more than friends with benefits. I remember talking to a friend's frat brother within a few days of dating Nancy. His two main questions punched me out. He wanted to know why I decided to pursue Nancy and what was wrong with you." Holt's voice trailed off as he finished speaking.

"Did you ever find an answer?" Torrey placed her feet firmly on the floor and quit fidgeting.

"Yes, after a lot of thought and introspection. It took me awhile. Here's what I came to understand. Nancy represented the wilder side of me. The me that wanted to sow his oats, as Gwen calls it. And a part of me wanted to be free. Settling down scared the shit out of me."

"I see. And what about now?"

Holt snorted. "Darlin', I realized that what scared the shit out of me more was losing you. Not having the one person I could talk to besides Stuart about anything and everything. You filled in the places he couldn't and never would."

"Why didn't you tell me this then?" Torrey's gaze locked with his.

"If you'd been accessible, I might have. I noticed the signals and figured you moved on. You were dating someone else by then I heard." Holt rocked back on his heels, shoved his hands into his pockets, and shrugged.

Torrey's shake of her head and sneer cut into him. God, was he losing her again?

Holt moved to his chair. He pulled the chair behind him, not halting until he was toe-to-toe with Torrey. He sat and took her hands in his. "No other woman ever came close to you and I doubt any ever will. I can't promise a future free of pain. I can only give you my word, I will do the very best I can to not cause you that kind of pain again."

Holt searched Torrey's face for a sign. Her blank stare drummed up more fear and worry than if she'd come out and said no. Holt raised her hand to his lips. He kissed each knuckle before turning her hand over. "I'm putting my heart and myself in your hand. Please say you'll take good care of us and my love for you."

Torrey blinked back renewed tears. This time joy flowed through her without barriers. She nodded, working her hands free from Holt's. She stood, holding her arms wide open. "I'm offering my heart freely. I can't hold back what I feel, either. I love you, Holt Addison."

Holt swooped her up into his arms. He spun them around before dizzily making his way to an empty chair. As he sat, he spoke. "I love you, Torrey

Neadson. I may forget to compromise and ask before I do. Please know I do this out of love and not being some Neanderthal."

Torrey giggled as Holt nibbled her neck. "Speaking of compromise. You know, we never did come to one concerning your actions when Bert came to the door."

Holt's ragged breath and sigh told Torrey he'd caught her emphasis on every word. She leaned back and took ahold of his chin. His eyes met hers. Moments seemed to pass as they regarded each other. Holt's breathing slowed. His nod at first was imperceptible and it became firmer with each subsequent bob. "I protect those I love and care about. I've got to realize they can and will do the same for me. A new thing for me. A very different way of seeing and doing."

"Yes, for us both. I've got to think about two and not just me. I've got changes to make, too. Growth for us both." Torrey brushed her lips over Holt's.

Holt slid his arms around her waist. "We'll work on it together. We're partners, okay?"

Torrey smiled and nodded before burying her face in Holt's shirt. Inhaling his musky masculine scent, she pushed her hands under his shirt, enjoying the warmth he gave off each time she kissed his chest. They still had things to learn about each other, possibly an obstacle or two to overcome together. The unknown would come, and whatever came, they would face it as partners.

Chapter Twenty-Five

A week and a half later

Everyone in the church turned as the ceremonial music started. Holt sidestepped closer to Stuart. They grinned as Graham, Mitch, and Terrence followed. Each of them looked sharp in their personal tux selections. Stuart decided that since each of them wanted to pay for their rental that they had a choice in what they wore. None ended up with tails or obnoxious-colored cummerbunds.

Holt smiled and nodded as Stuart whispered to him. "Look, here comes Torrey. Man, she looks radiant."

"Yes, she does." Holt's smile reached his eyes and grew in intensity the closer Torrey got. Her dress fell just below her knee. Each time she walked, the skirt rippled and move with her. Even the low heels she wore added elegance to her. Her hair curled around her face, creating a halo. The simple mauve rose mixed with baby's breath tucked into her hair added to the touches of mauve in her bouquet and shawl. She stepped up and stood in place as Joanna's attendants each took their place behind her as they came down the aisle.

Abebi stumbled a couple of times on her way down the aisle. Poor thing hadn't had much time to acclimate to girly frills and feminine shoes. Holt grabbed Mitch's arm to keep him from rescuing her. He needed to let her handle the situation. Then there were the last two women who made their way to the altar without issue. Terrence eyed one of them and sighed. Graham had his eyes on all the women. He wouldn't comment on who looked lovelier or better. Holt suspected he had his own agenda.

A whispered "Oh, look how cute" cut the silence in between changes in music pieces. Twin small girls skipped down the aisle, tossing rose petals out of their baskets as they approached the front of the church. Their male cousin followed behind them, wearing a regal smile and holding, far out in front of him, a pillow bearing two wedding bands. Two steps from the altar area, he tripped. Mitch caught him in time to keep the rings on the pillow. Holt could hear everyone's, including his, sigh of relief.

The bridal processional sounded. The rear doors of the sanctuary opened. Two ushers entered, holding the doors as the music grew in volume. Through them stepped first Joanna's mother with Stuart's mother, each of them holding lit candles. The candles matched the bride's colors. Right behind them came Grandma Getty on Stuart's father's arm. She beamed and nodded to those she knew. Holt bit his lip as her gaze caught his. He swore she winked at him. The old gal had her moments. She loved and cared for her flock as if they were all hers, whether they were blood related or not. Once she said to call her grandma, that person became family for life. Holt hoped she stayed around for quite a few more years. He wanted his children to know Grandma Getty.

A hush fell over the sanctuary as all rose. Holt leaned out a bit and knew why Stuart and Joanna had insisted on casual clothes at the rehearsal. All her attendants radiated in their apparel. No one could stand up to Joanna and the smile she wore as she made her way down the aisle on her father's arm. Her simple-cut dress matched in style to her attendants. The rich, silky beige color with mauve accents stood out and framed her as if she and the dress were one. Her veil complemented the dress with its antique lace. Bless Grandma Getty and Joanna's mom for coming up with the idea for the veil. Something old and treasured made part of the wedding. The two women had lovingly made the veil out of their own bridal veils. Holt glanced at Torrey. Her eyes locked with his.

Torrey knew the moment she entered the sanctuary that her decision was correct and right for her. The last two weeks were intense and revealing. Holt had spent almost every night with her, whether it was at her place or his. They found themselves discussing aspects of ritual and things of importance that neither had touched upon before. Compromise had happened naturally with them. Holt talked about why he had chosen law school as his way to return to the community what they had seen in him. Several local scholarships assisted him through his undergrad and grad studies. He learned how important roots and home were to her. They both agreed Cascade Bay was their first choice for both. While neither of them had verbally said it, most of their friends and extended family assumed they were a couple. Even Grandma Getty smiled when she saw the two of them together. Torrey knew the future held risk and many unknowns as she and Holt went forward. With Holt by her side, Torrey didn't see bleak things occurring.

Torrey tried to look away, but she couldn't. Holt looked delicious in his tuxedo. How long did she have to wait until she could touch him and nibble his neck as they danced? At the rehearsal dinner, they held hands under the table and danced together as the younger group gathered at McClark's afterward for a night of merriment. With the lights down low, Holt had whispered in her ear as he nipped it what he planned to do her once the wedding and reception were over. Torrey shivered as potential images came to mind. Who knew a little restraint and ice could produce such carnal delights?

Joanna cleared her throat as she handed Torrey her bouquet. "Keep focused for about thirty minutes more. Then you can ogle Holt all you want."

Torrey blushed and ducked her head. She glanced up as Joanna leaned down and kissed her cheek. "I didn't think it was that obvious."

Joanna replied before turning. "Even Grandma Getty says you two are next to jump the broomstick."

Torrey caught her smile and knowing wink. Holt winked at her as she looked at him. Had he read Joanna's lips or hers?

As Joanna and Stuart re-exchanged their vows, Torrey observed the friends and family in attendance. Back toward the last few pews in the church, her parents sat. Torrey swallowed hard. They glowed when they smiled. Her dad sat with his arm around her mother, hugging her close as Joanna and Stuart said, "I do." It was if they reaffirmed their own vows. How tight and close everyone was considering how large Cascade Bay had grown. Torrey knew she wanted to continue calling this place home now and in the future. Would Holt feel the same way?

True to her word, Joanna and Stuart turned almost twenty minutes later, facing their guests as the deacon introduced them as husband and wife. Torrey laughed with the rest as the deacon mentioned his twenty-first century thinking and called them by their names rather than Mr. and Mrs. Doxson. As applause and cheers broke out, Joanna accepted her bouquet from Torrey. The recessional music sounded, and Holt offered Torrey his arm. His conspiratorial wink and quick grin sent ripples warping through her stomach. He patted her hand and whisked her out of the sanctuary right behind Stuart and Joanna. As the receiving line formed in the narthex, Holt kissed Torrey not once but twice. More cheers and applause broke out as they parted. What was with him?

Torrey opened her mouth to chastise Holt when he kissed her again. This time a full-out French kiss. Several throats cleared, and Torrey peeked over Holt's shoulder. Her dad gazed back at her over his glasses. Her mother smiled as she patted her hand that wore her wedding band.

Holt brushed his lips across Torrey's cheek. "Love, you blush so well," he whispered before facing the first guests exiting the chapel.

As the guests filed out and down the line, Holt patted his pocket. He felt the small lump within. The box fit in his hand if he reached in and palmed it. The size and roundness were right. Exactly what the lady had said her favorite gem and design were. He hoped her reaction was positive.

"Come on, love. Let's get to the car before the rest decide to block us in. I had to park way back in the parking lot." Holt grabbed Torrey's hand and hurried her down the stairs. A cool wind blew in off the bay. Only a few clouds filled the light-blue sky. Even the water seemed bluer as the sun shone on it. Holt took off his jacket and draped it across Torrey shoulders as they trotted to his car.

Halfway across the parking lot, the limo stopped near them. The window rolled down and Stuart leaned out. "Think you two can behave and make it to the reception hall?"

Joanna waved them closer. She called out, "Yes, no rumbled clothes, please. Remember, eyes are on us." Her laughter rang forth as Stuart closed the window.

Holt laughed as Torrey blushed more. "Come on, love. We've got a reception to attend."

Epilogue

Three hours later

Holt pulled Torrey tighter to him. Dinner and toasts were done. Many of the older guests gathered, talking as the musicians started in with the slow music of the night. Stuart and Joanna danced near them. Even Stuart's dad got Grandma Getty out to bossa nova with the middle-aged guests. Grandma could still cut a mean rug. Halfway through the song, the lead vocal called out for partners to switch. Torrey found herself dancing with Stuart. He held her a safe distance from him. Five minutes later, *change partners* rang out again. Laughter flowed as some of the older guests snuck onto the dance floor. Joanna stood in front of Torrey, hiked up her skirt a bit, and started doing the Charleston. Torrey joined in and had others lining up with them. As time passed, other songs, fast and slow, filled the air. Torrey found herself back with Holt as a fast number ended. Fanning herself, she led the way back to their table.

"Lord, I didn't know Grandma had that much get-up-and-go. She danced for quite a while. Stuart and Joanna are seeing her off now. Too bad she'll miss the cake cutting." Torrey drank part of her water.

"I know. She wanted to stay but was getting more tired by the moment. She was up before dawn finishing the cake. Wait until Stuart and Joanna see it." Holt held out the chair so Torrey could sit.

"Please tell me she kept it simple. Joanna will never live down an elaborate cake. It just isn't her." Torrey entwined her fingers with Holt's.

Holt raised their hands to his lips. He kissed each knuckle, working his way to her wrist. He stopped and raised his head. "The cake is as simple as what is in my pocket. Can you get it out for me? And I mean my jacket pocket."

Torrey laughed. "Why can't you get it out of your pocket?" She leaned closer.

"Because I don't want to let go of your hand. Just help me out okay? Please." Holt did his best male imitation of batting his eyelashes at Torrey.

Torrey muffled her laughter by biting her lip. "Yes, I'll help you." She leaned against him and slid her hand over his abdomen, taking a few moments of pleasure to sneak her fingers inside his shirt.

"Behave, woman. We're in public. You can undress me later. When we're alone and out of view. With the bedroom door closed. Siam, Mischa, and Doxie can sleep in the living room tonight." Holt hissed as Torrey dragged her hand down his torso to his thigh. "Pocket, love. Jacket pocket, remember, not pants."

"Do I have to?" Torrey slowly stroked up his leg, reaching his hip.

"Yes, for now. On to the jacket pocket, please." The imp was loving every moment. She knew he wanted to take her home and spend the rest of the evening and night pleasuring them both.

Torrey patted down Holt's jacket until she felt the object inside. "Lord that is a small box. I think I'm gonna need both hands to get it out, okay."

Holt let go of her hand. "Do what you need to." He held his arms wide open. Torrey smirked as she stuck both hands into the pocket. She fumbled with the box as she placed it on the table. An ornate bow matching her dress encircled the box. A tag with her name in calligraphy hung down the side.

Torrey looked up at Holt. "Is this what I think it is?"

Holt shrugged. "Could be. Why not open it and make sure?"

Torrey's hand shook as she took ahold of the bow. Two tugs and the ribbon fell to the table. Holt reached over and his hand covered hers. "Maybe you need help."

Holt picked up the box and acted as though he was going to open it. "Wait, I need to take this jacket off. It's beginning to bother me." He stood. Instead of taking his jacket off, he dropped to one knee.

"Will you," he began, opening the box, "spend the rest of your life with me?"

Torrey blinked. Tears of joy streamed down her cheeks. Her prayers were heard, and her guardian angels knew her heart's desire. There was only one answer. "Yes, my love. My past, present, and future love. Yes."

Holt slipped the diamond and amethyst gemmed ring on her finger and drew her to him as he stood. Their song began playing. A spotlight shown on the dance floor. Stuart and Joanna joined them under it. In the background, the lead vocal started singing "To Love Somebody" by the Bee Gees. The lyrics rang true for each couple present.

THE END

WWW.SOLARAGORDON.COM

Don't miss out!

Visit the website below and you can sign up to receive emails whenever Solara Gordon publishes a new book. There's no charge and no obligation.

https://books2read.com/r/B-A-RAUJ-GEZOB

BOOKS 2 READ

Connecting independent readers to independent writers.

Did you love *Love Reborn*? Then you should read *A Heart's Desire*[1] by Solara Gordon!

[2]

With his sister's engagement party and wedding looming, Parker needs a date if he's to avoid having his sister and mother set him up with someone. The one person at the top of his list to ask is also the same woman he's fought his attraction to. Worse, they work together. Is it worth problems at work if she turns him down? What if she realizes he wants to be more than a co-worker?

Every time Parker walks into work, Angela struggles to hide her growing attraction to her co-worker. Now the delicious hunk of a man she's watched from the start, a man who can have any woman he wants, asks her out? When a heavy spring snowstorm forces them to take shelter at Parker's townhouse, will they push past their fears of rejection, or let this opportunity slip away?

Read more at https://solaragordon.com/.

---

1. https://books2read.com/u/4DyZED

2. https://books2read.com/u/4DyZED

Also by Solara Gordon

Cascade Bay
Love Reborn

Standalone
A Heart's Desire
To Love You Again
To Love You Again

Watch for more at https://solaragordon.com/.

About the Author

Solara loves and lives with her partner of 21 years in the Metro DC area. What started out as a bi-coastal romance soon settled on one coast.

A vivid imagination keeps her busy creating her next fascinating romance. She enjoys creating unique characters and watching their journeys unfold. "Love freely given multiplies and will return endlessly" is a key aspect of her stories. Add in alternative lifestyles and her love for the paranormal, and the uncommon becomes the norm in many of her stories.

Her day job in the financial services industry pays the bills while she pens her erotic tales.

Read more at https://solaragordon.com/.